"This isn't a g

"I think it's a great
wicked, innocent, s

He clenched his jaw again. "That's because you don't know better," he told her. "I'm too old for you."

"Too old," she echoed. "That's crazy. It's not as if you're twenty years older."

"Trust me, cupcake," he said. "I feel like I'm eighty years older."

Angie rolled her eyes. "You exaggerate. You're just finding your feet and way. That's why you feel unsure."

"I don't know about that," Forrest said.

"Well, I do," she said in a husky whisper as she leaned toward him.

"You need to leave," he said.

"Isn't that a bit drastic?" she asked.

"Not at all," he said, and steeled himself not to respond to her.

"Just one more kiss," she whispered in an inviting voice.

"No," he said, but it killed him.

Dear Reader,

I loved being a part of this wonderful Montana Mavericks series. Forrest Traub, the hero in my story, has returned from Iraq and is recovering from an injury where he almost lost his leg. He also struggles with post-traumatic stress disorder. I had the opportunity to talk with a soldier who'd lost most of his rib cage from a gunshot wound, and he also suffered from PTSD. The adjustments he had to face after his injuries were unbelievably challenging. I was grateful to hear that the military offers support and actual techniques for how to deal with PTSD.

In my story, the hero displays a different kind of courage by starting a support group for war veterans. Have you noticed that struggling with a problem by yourself makes it feel so much bigger than if you share it with someone who cares? Forrest Traub may be a courageous man, yet between his bum leg and his nightmares and hypervigilance, he believes he's in no shape for a committed relationship. Angie Anderson, however, is like a burst of sunshine on Forrest's dark soul. But can she turn his jaded heart around? Maybe a little holiday magic can help them along.

Wishing you all the joy of the holidays,

Leanne Banks

A MAVERICK FOR THE HOLIDAYS

LEANNE BANKS

HARLEQUIN®
entertain, enrich, inspire™

Special thanks and acknowledgment to Leanne Banks
for her contribution to the
Montana Mavericks: Back in the Saddle continuity.

Recycling programs
for this product may
not exist in your area.

ISBN-13: 978-0-373-65704-9

A MAVERICK FOR THE HOLIDAYS

Copyright © 2012 by Harlequin Books S.A.

This edition published by arrangement with Harlequin Books S.A.

For questions and comments about the quality of this book,
please contact us at CustomerService@Harlequin.com.

www.Harlequin.com

Printed in U.S.A.

Books by Leanne Banks

Harlequin Special Edition

The Prince's Texas Bride #2115
The Doctor Takes a Princess #2127
§*A Maverick for Christmas* #2151
††*The Princess and the Outlaw* #2198
††*A Home for Nobody's Princess* #2216
§§*A Maverick for the Holidays* #2222

Silhouette Special Edition

Royal Holiday Baby #2075

*The Royal Dumonts
†The Billionaires Club
**The Medici Men
§Montana Mavericks:
   The Texans Are Coming!
††Royal Babies
§§Montana Mavericks:
   Back in the Saddle!

Silhouette Desire

His Majesty, M.D. #1435
The Playboy & Plain Jane #1483
Princess in His Bed #1515
Between Duty and Desire #1599
Shocking the Senator #1621
Billionaire's Proposition #1699
†*Bedded by the Billionaire* #1863
†*Billionaire's Marriage
   Bargain* #1886
*Blackmailed Into a Fake
   Engagement* #1916
Billionaire Extraordinaire #1939
From Playboy to Papa! #1987
**The Playboy's Proposition* #1995
**Secrets of the Playboy's Bride* #2002
CEO's Expectant Secretary #2018

Other titles by Leanne Banks
available in ebook format.

LEANNE BANKS

is a *New York Times* and *USA TODAY* bestselling author who is surprised every time she realizes how many books she has written. Leanne loves chocolate, the beach and new adventures. To name a few, Leanne has ridden on an elephant, stood on an ostrich egg (no, it didn't break), and gone parasailing and indoor skydiving. Leanne loves writing romance because she believes in the power and magic of love. She lives in Virginia with her family and a four-and-a-half-pound Pomeranian named Bijou. Visit her website, www.leannebanks.com.

This book is dedicated to all the veterans
who've returned from hostile countries
who continue to battle post-traumatic stress disorder
and to those who love them.

Prologue

The truck they were driving was loaded with artillery, but there were several more in the caravan. In his position as major, Forrest normally wouldn't have been traveling, but there had been complaints about getting signatures for the items they were transporting. In the army, it was always about getting signatures, even here in the desert of Iraq. Enough crap about signatures, they had a war to win.

Suddenly, an explosion ripped through the vehicle. Everything blurred. Forrest raced out of the Humvee. A shot hit him in his armored vest. Another hit his leg. Again and again. His leg screamed in pain.

Out of the corner of his eye, he saw a soldier fall to the ground, then another and another. He tried to crawl to help them, but his leg was dead.

He was dead.

Forrest woke up in a sweat, his heart pounding in his chest, adrenaline racing. He reached for his weapon, but it wasn't there. He blinked and his eyes finally adjusted to the darkness. He wasn't in Iraq. He was in Montana. He wondered if he'd yelled, and prayed he hadn't. He didn't want his brother to know that he was still messed up. He didn't want anyone to know that his head was more broken than his leg was.

He wondered if he would always feel as if he were riding the edge of insanity. *Crazy*, he must be crazy.

Snippets of his therapy skittered through his brain.

You're not crazy. When you wake up from a night-mare or flashback, remind yourself that you're not crazy.

Practice your breathing technique.

Forrest inhaled and counted as he exhaled. *Controlled breathing will make you feel more in control of yourself.* Forrest continued the technique he'd been taught. He touched the quilt on his bed and rose, dragging his near-useless leg with him across the wooden floor to the bathroom.

Turning on the faucet, he washed his hands. The

water felt cold and it took the memories a little further away from him. He stuck his cup under the running water and lifted it to his mouth, taking several swallows.

When would his nightmare end?

Chapter One

Forrest wrapped up his quick meeting with Annabel Cates, Thunder Canyon's librarian and therapy-dog owner. "I'm glad we're starting this group for veterans. Sometimes it's just easier to talk when you're petting a dog," he said and couldn't resist giving Smiley, Annabel's therapy dog, a quick rub.

Annabel smiled in return. "I'm sure Smiley will love all the attention. Why don't you take him for a walk? He's been cooped up in here all morning."

Forrest nodded and accepted the leash of the gentle golden retriever. "Sounds like a good plan to me."

As he stepped outside the library door, the cold November air hit him with a snap. He inhaled and the sensation was so sharp it was almost painful, but the sun was shining brightly and Smiley was wagging his big furry tail so hard it was banging against Forrest's good leg. The dog's happiness gave him a lift and he led the golden down the street. One of the nice things about Smiley was he was trained so well that he never pulled on the leash. The dog followed his lead, and with Forrest's bum leg, that made the walk a lot more pleasurable.

Forrest crossed the street and relaxed a smidge. With Smiley, he'd noticed one of the symptoms of his PTSD—the docs called it hypervigilance—diminished just a little. Always nice to get a break from feeling like he needed to be ready for incoming fire any minute.

Forrest turned down another street, liking the way he was starting to feel at home in town. After his medical discharge from the army, he'd hoped that going back to the family ranch in Rust Creek Falls would help, but it hadn't. Everything he'd once done with ease underscored his new limitations with his injured leg. Forrest glanced down and noticed that his shoelace was untied. With his iffy balance, he sure as hell didn't want to trip over it. Awkwardly bending down, he began to retie it.

Suddenly Smiley let out a bark and raced away from him. Forrest reached for the leash, but it slid from his grasp. He swore under his breath. His heart raced in his chest. What if Smiley got hurt? He'd never forgive himself.

"Smiley," he yelled. "Smiley." Stumbling after the galloping golden retriever, he walked down the street as fast as he could.

A young woman appeared out of a doorway and stood directly in Smiley's path. Forrest feared the dog would knock her down. "Smiley," he called again.

"Smiley! Sit," the woman said.

Wonder of wonders, the therapy dog plopped his bottom on the pavement and wagged his tail, with his tongue hanging out the side of his mouth.

Relief rushed through Forrest as he finally caught up with the dog. "Thanks for stopping him," Forrest said, grabbing his breath at the same time as he grabbed the leash. "I was afraid he was going to run into that traffic."

The girl shrugged her shoulders. "It was nothing. I guess he just wanted to come over and say hello."

"Do you know him?" Forrest asked, still perplexed that Smiley had taken off like that.

The girl studied Smiley for a moment. "Based on that therapy vest, I'm guessing he belongs to Annabel Cates. My sister Haley is married to Marlon Cates and he's Annabel's brother, but I have to say I've never actually met the dog before."

"That's weird, because Smiley headed over here like he knew where he was going," he said, taking a second look at the girl. He couldn't exactly nail her age, but she looked young. Her brown hair flowed past her shoulders and her eyes were big and brown, glinting with happiness. She made him feel a little old.

The girl laughed lightly and the sound felt like a cool drink of water on a hot day. "Maybe this dog is just super smart and knew that ROOTS is a great place to hang out," she said, pointing to the sign in the window. She gave him an appraising look. "Wait a minute. Are you related to Rose Traub?"

"Yeah, she's my cousin. Why?"

"Rose is married to my brother Austin. I'm Angie Anderson," she said and extended her hand.

"Forrest Traub. Man, this is one small town. Seems like most everyone is related," he said.

"You're right about that. Why don't you come inside? We've got hot chocolate and cookies," she said.

"That's okay. I better get Smiley back to Annabel," he said.

"I'm sure Smiley could use a little rest after the way he was racing down the street," she said.

His leg was aching like hell, so he decided he could use a break. "If you're sure," he said. "What do you do here, anyway?" he asked as he followed her inside.

"I'm a volunteer," she said. "ROOTS is a safe haven for the local youth."

"But aren't you a youth?" he couldn't help asking because Angie looked so young.

She laughed again, and the sound just made him feel better. "I guess I'll accept that as a compliment," she said. "I'm twenty-three and going to college. I work here at ROOTS part-time. How do you like your hot chocolate? Light or loaded on the marshmallows?" she asked.

He almost chuckled at the way she asked. "Light. The bad thing about a sugar high is what comes afterward," he said.

"Coming right up. Have a seat," she said and went to a snack and beverage table at the far end of the room.

"Hey," a teenage boy with long hair said, stepping toward Smiley. "Cool dog. Can I pet him?"

"Sure can. He's a therapy dog, so he's trained to be friendly. He may need a little refresher course, though," Forrest said wryly, giving the golden an affectionate rub.

"What do you mean?" the teenager asked, bending down to pet Smiley.

"He took off while I was walking him today, and he's not supposed to do that," Forrest said.

"So he's in trouble?" the teenager asked.

"His mistress will have to make that call," Forrest said.

Angie returned with a cup of hot chocolate. "What do you think of Smiley, Max?"

"He's a cool dog. You should bring him around more often," he said. "Oh, look, Lilly's here. We're gonna do some homework together."

"Okay, I'll be right here if you need any help," Angie said and sat next to Forrest. When Max took a few steps away, she shot Forrest a mischievous look. "I don't know how much actual homework they'll get done. Max has a monster crush on Lilly," she said in a low voice.

Forrest glanced at the teenage boy and girl as they sat at a table together and felt a pinch of loss. He shook his head. "Sometimes I wonder if I was ever that young."

"Well, you're not ancient," she said. "It's not like you can remember when electricity was invented."

This time he did chuckle. "I guess. It's just been a long road since I got back from Iraq."

Angie's eyes widened. "You were in Iraq?"

"Yeah, army. I enlisted after high school and earned my engineering degree before my first tour of Iraq. My second tour ended my military career," he said and took a drink of hot chocolate. "I hadn't planned on that. An IED took me out of action."

"IED?" she echoed.

"Improvised explosive device."

"That must have been horrible."

"It was worse for some than others. I was in the first vehicle, so we took the brunt of it."

"So, you're a hero," she said, her gaze intent.

"Oh, no," he said, feeling self-conscious at the admiring expression in her eyes. "Just doing my job."

"I'm sure plenty of people would agree with me. How long will you be in town?" she asked.

"A while," he said. "There's a doc here who's going to do some more work on my leg. Plus I've started doing blueprints for an architectural firm. What about you?" he asked, ready for the attention to be taken off of him.

"I'm hoping to finish my bachelor's degree in sociology within the next year. I work in the college administration office one day a week. I temp for a CPA during tax season and work part-time for a catering business. And like I mentioned, I volunteer here at ROOTS and for some other charities," she said and her cheeks turned pink. "I really don't know what I want to do for the rest of my life," she confessed. "I wish I did. I wish it would just hit me on the head like it seems to do for other people, but so far, it hasn't. But I'm not going to sit home waiting to find out, so I stay pretty busy."

"Jill-of-all-trades," he said.

"Huh?" she asked, furrowing her brow in confusion.

"As opposed to jack-of-all-trades. You're a jill-of-all-trades," he said.

She gave a slow smile that had a surprising edge of sexiness. "I like that. I'm glad Smiley led you to stop here today."

Forrest felt flattered at the same time that a mental alarm went off. Angie might not be a teenager, but she was still too young for him, so he sure as hell didn't want to give her any ideas. "Thanks for lassoing Smiley and giving me some hot chocolate. I should walk him back to the library now," he said, rising. Pain shot through his leg, but he gritted his teeth so no one would see.

"There's no need to rush off," she said, bobbing to her feet.

He couldn't prevent a twist of envy at how easy it was for her to move around. Those days were gone for him. At least for the present. "I really should go. Thanks again," he said. "You take care."

She met his gaze. "You, too. Who knows? It's a small town. We may see each other again."

Making a noncommittal sound, he made his way out the door to the sidewalk. He glanced back at the doorway and caught sight of Angie waving at him. He waved in return and walked away.

She was a cute girl. In the same way a sister was cute, he told himself. She was the exact opposite of him. He was a busted-up retired army major. Most days, he felt like he was eighty-years-old.

Angie had the lively glint of a *very* young woman who hasn't seen the ugly side of life. He envied her innocence, and he couldn't ever imagine being as open as she was. Not now. Not after everything he'd seen and experienced.

He took the short walk to the library and led Smiley inside.

Annabel smiled and greeted both of them. "Smiley, boy, good to see you. And to you, too, Forrest. How did Smiley do?"

"Pretty good except when he ran off," he said, giving her the leash.

Annabel's face fell. "Ran off?" she echoed and glanced at her dog. "When did he do that?"

"About halfway through the walk, he took off toward ROOTS. Maybe he was drumming up business for himself," he said.

Annabel gave a half laugh, but he could tell she wasn't really amused. "Maybe. He's trained not to run away."

"Angie Anderson stopped him. Good thing. I was afraid he would get hit by a car."

Annabel winced. "I don't know why he did that. Thank goodness for Angie," she said, rubbing Smiley's neck.

"True," he said. "What do you know about her?"

"The Andersons are a great family," Anabel said. "They've had some tough times, but Angie really came through it well."

"She seems too young to be working at that youth center."

"ROOTS?" Anabel said. "They actually like having some younger volunteers. It helps the kids identify with a good role model. I hear Angie's a sweet, easygoing girl."

Forrest shrugged, backing off. He shouldn't be curious about Angie. "Okay. I'll head on back home now. Thanks for the adventure," he said.

She bit her lip. "I feel bad that he ran off on you."

"It wasn't a problem," he said. "I caught up to him."

"Well," Annabel said. "I think Smiley is due for some retraining, and I'll start tonight."

Forrest nodded. "You'll figure it out," he said. "You've done a great job with him."

"Thanks," Annabel said. "But he'll be even better next time you see him!"

Angie forced her attention back to the kids at ROOTS, but she couldn't help thinking about Forrest. Talking with him had made her feel as if someone had lit a lamp inside her. A few other guys had temporarily captured her attention, but she knew that Forrest was totally different from them. It seemed as if every cell in her body was screaming how special he could be to her. The strength of her instant attraction to him was distracting.

As she cleaned up the snack station near the end of her shift, Lilly Evans approached her. Lilly was a beautiful serious-minded seventeen-year-old with long blond hair and green eyes. Lilly had been active in ROOTS during the last two years since her father had gone to prison. Angie admired the girl for keeping her focus during such a traumatic time.

"Hey, there," Angie said. "How'd the study time go with Max?"

Lilly shrugged. "I'm not sure. He doesn't seem to concentrate very well."

Angie chuckled. "That could be because he's got a crush on you."

Lilly's pale cheeks bloomed with color. "I don't have time for that," she said. "Too many other things going on."

Angie heard an undertone of anxiety in Lilly's voice. "Like what?" she asked.

"My mother's afraid she's going to lose her main job, so she's started working another one part-time."

"The economy is hard on a lot of people right now," Angie said and squeezed Lilly's shoulder. "I hope she'll get some good news soon."

"Me, too. If that weren't bad enough, my brother

Joey has been hanging around some bad kids. I'm worried about him."

"How old is he?" Angie asked. "Maybe you could bring him to ROOTS."

"He's thirteen, but he doesn't think ROOTS is cool," she said, rolling her eyes.

"What else is he interested in?" Angie asked.

"Violent computer games," Lilly said with a frown. "He shoots basketball every now and then. He's a little on the skinny side, so I think he tries to act all tough." She sighed. "We had a dog for a while and Joey really liked him, but my dad made us give him away."

"Hmm," Angie murmured, her mind working. "What about working at the animal shelter? We have a group that volunteers there twice a month. If he really likes it, he could go more often on his own. In the meantime, if he goes with the ROOTS group, he'll be exposed to some different kids and maybe make some better friends."

"That's a great idea," Lilly said. "If we can just figure out how to get him to go."

"If you want, I can have one of the ROOTS shelter volunteers give him a call. I can call him, too."

"That might help, but he still could turn you down. Joey can be stubborn."

"We'll wear him down," Angie said. "I'll have the ROOTS coordinator contact him first."

Lilly sighed. "Thanks. I'm really worried about him."

"We'll give this a try and see how it works. Make sure you're keeping your mother up to speed, and if she needs extra help, we're in touch with some wonderful counselors. Some of them even offer a couple free sessions."

Lilly impulsively threw her arms around Angie and Angie hugged her in return. "Remember you're not alone, here," Angie said and gave the teen a reassuring squeeze. Her heart broke for the trauma Lilly had experienced during the last few years. It was hard always being the strong one. Angie was so grateful that Lilly trusted her enough to talk to her.

After her shift, Angie left ROOTS and walked into her empty home. Since her brother Austin and sister Haley had left, she was all alone. Angie spent as little time at home as possible. She knew she was fortunate to have a rent-free home, but the silence that welcomed her every night disturbed her. After today, she had a feeling she might not be alone forever. She had a very strong feeling about Forrest Traub. So strong she couldn't keep it to herself.

Even though she could have called Haley earlier when she was at ROOTS, Angie had held off. But now she couldn't. She dialed her sister's cell and waited, her heart racing.

"Hey," Haley said. "How are you doing?"

"Great," Angie said and took a deep breath. "And I've just met the most amazing man today. His name is Forrest Traub. He's a veteran and he's the man of my dreams."

Haley chuckled. "And you know this after one meeting?" she asked.

"I do," Angie said, wandering around the den. "He's everything I've ever wanted. He's the man I always wanted without knowing that I wanted him. Haley, he's not a boy. He's a man and he's strong and he has a good heart. You should have seen him with that therapy dog."

"Therapy dog?" Haley echoed.

"He was taking Annabel's dog Smiley for a walk. Of course, it doesn't hurt that he's hot. But I can tell there's much more to him."

"If you say so," Haley said.

"I do," Angie insisted.

"Okay, that's exciting," Haley said.

Angie could hear Haley's disbelief and it bothered her. "You're patronizing me," Angie said.

"I'm not," Haley said. "Give me a chance. I haven't met the guy."

Angie sighed. "Okay. Fair enough."

"Good," Haley said. "Are you doing okay?"

Angie glanced around the den of the house and fought the sense of loneliness. "I'm good. Keeping busy," she said as she paced.

"You should come to visit us for dinner more often," Haley said.

"You're a newlywed. I don't want to intrude," Angie said.

"It's not an intrusion," Haley countered.

"Seems like it to me. I don't want to crash a honeymoon," Angie said.

Haley chuckled. "Just give us a few minutes' notice and we're good."

"I feel so much better," Angie teased.

Silence followed. "Sweetie, you know we are here for you."

"Yeah, I know," Angie said.

"We love you," Haley said.

"Love you, too," Angie returned and hung up her phone.

Taking a deep breath, she meandered from the doorway to the kitchen. A dozen memories flashed through her mind. Her brother making pancakes for her breakfast. Haley helping her get ready for prom.

Angie knew that Haley and Austin had worked their butts off to make up for the fact that their father had left soon after she'd been born and her mother had died during her early teens.

The great blessing had been that both her sister and brother had found true love. They'd moved out of the house to make their new lives with their loves. Angie couldn't be happier, except for the fact that she was now alone. And she didn't always quite know what to do with herself.

Austin and Haley checked in on her frequently, but Angie didn't want to be a burden. After all, she was twenty-three. She should be fully capable of managing her life.

But the house felt so silent. It was too quiet. Stalking into the den, she grabbed the remote for the television and turned it on. She didn't care about the program. She just wanted the sound of human voices. Returning to the kitchen, she pulled out a frozen dinner, zapped it in the microwave and took it with her into the den.

She sank onto the sofa and pulled out the notebook she kept for her charity projects. With the holidays approaching, she knew her schedule would get busier. Somehow more kids seemed to show up at ROOTS during the holidays, which meant the youth center needed more adults manning different shifts. She would juggle that with working several holiday dinners and parties for the catering company that kept her bank account healthy.

Angie had also learned from her sister, Haley, that helping other people made her less likely to feel sorry for herself. That was why she liked to get the ROOTS kids to contribute to a charity activity. It didn't have to require money, just some time and effort. The kids learned that it was rewarding to give of themselves.

Her mind turned to thoughts of Forrest Traub as she jotted thoughts in her notebook. She drew a military emblem. She wondered how he had survived the attack. It sounded like it must have been horrible. Yet, she could tell he was no quitter. He was the type of man determined to make the best of his situation. She suspected he was the kind to surpass everyone's expectations.

An idea fluttered through her mind. Maybe the ROOTS group could do something to benefit the military. But what?

The next morning, Forrest woke up early. Too early. He turned to one of the few things that brought him solace—working out. Exercise made his body stronger. He could only hope it would eventually. He'd set up a home gym in the second bedroom of his suite at the boardinghouse. Since his brother Clay had fallen in love with their landlord, Clay and his baby son, Bennett, had moved out and were staying in the main house with Antonia and her baby, Lucy. Clay and Antonia would be getting married very soon. Although Forrest was happy for his brother, he couldn't help feeling overwhelmed by how quiet his place was now that his brother had left.

Forrest lifted weights. His cell phone rang, surprising him. He didn't recognize the number, but noticed it was local. "Forrest Traub," he said.

"Hi, Forrest," a breathless feminine voice said. "This is Angie Anderson."

Whoa, he thought and set down his weights. "Hi, how are you?"

"I'm fine," she said. "How are you?"

"Pretty good," he replied and began to pace. "How can I help you?"

"Thank you for the offer," she said with a laugh. "I have an idea. I think it would be great if the ROOTS kids got involved in a GI holiday pen pal program."

Forrest nodded. "Not a bad idea. You can get in touch with a national group—"

"I don't want to do that," she said. "I want to keep it more local, and I was hoping you could help me."

Surprise raced through him. "Me?"

"Yes, you. You would be perfect. You're a veteran. You could inspire the ROOTS group," she said.

Forrest shook his head. "I'm not sure—"

"I am," Angie said. "Let's get together and talk about it."

Forrest blinked. Sheesh. This woman moved fast. "I'm not coming into town today, so—"

"I can come to you," she said. "Where do you live?"

"Hey, that's not necessary," he said.

"It's no problem," she said. "Where do you live?"

He sighed and gave her the address. "You really don't need to do this," he said.

"It's *really* no problem. See you later. I'll bring lunch," she said and hung up before he could protest.

Forrest stared at his phone and had a bad premonition. This woman was going to be trouble.

A few hours later, he heard footfalls bounding up the steps to the front porch of the rooming house. Since he was currently the only occupant, he suspected that Angie was his visitor. He opened the door before she had a chance to knock and looked at her. The sight of her fresh beauty made something skitter under his skin. She looked so innocent, feminine and real.

"Hey," he said.

"Hey," she said with a broad smile in return. "Can I come in?"

"Sure," he said and noticed she was carrying a bag from a local sub shop. "You didn't need to bring food."

"I told you I would. If you can drum up some coffee or water, we're covered," she said.

"Okay," he said and led her inside the first-floor-level suite.

"This is nice," she said, looking around as she followed him inside.

He filled a couple glasses of water in the small kitchen and returned to her. "It fits my needs at the moment." He rubbed the back of his neck. "Listen, I may not be the best source for your pen pal idea. I left several months ago and I don't really know that many soldiers from around here."

"Oh, you don't have to help me with names. I can get those. No problem. What I want you to do is talk to the ROOTS group and tell them how good it felt to receive cards and letters of encouragement. Especially around the holidays." She jiggled her bag. "Do you want to eat in the kitchen?"

"There isn't much of one," he said. "I usually eat in here," he said, tilting his head toward the den area.

She gave a short chuckle. "You sound like me. Ever since I've been living alone, I eat my frozen meal in front of the TV. When I'm home, that is," she added as she sank onto the sofa. "Most of the time, I'm on the go."

"Why don't you get a roommate?" he asked.

"I don't know. I just haven't gotten around to it," she said. "Ever since I was thirteen, it was just my sister, brother and me. It feels strange now."

He wondered what had happened to her parents, but didn't want to pry. "I know what you're saying. Since my brother and Antonia got together and he moved into the main house, it's pretty quiet here."

"Well, maybe I can break down and fix a meal and you can come over to my place for dinner sometime," she said.

Even though Angie was cute as a button and clearly attracted to him, he didn't want to give her false hope. Forrest cleared his throat. "So what kind of sandwiches do you have in that bag?" he asked, deliberately avoiding her suggestion.

"Oh," she said. "I made a big guess that you're not a vegetarian and got you an Italian hero."

He laughed under his breath as he unwrapped the sandwich. "Good guess. Thanks."

She opened her notebook. "Now, I've done some research on the pen pal programs, and I think this will be very empowering for our ROOTS kids. So much of the time, they don't feel as if they have any control over their lives. Especially if they're having problems at home or school. This is a small thing they can do, and it's not a big commitment, but it has big impact on both the sender and the receiver. Don't you agree?"

Forrest hadn't really thought much about it, but he supposed it was true. Angie was so enthusiastic he felt like a heel at the thought of letting her down. "I guess so."

"I knew you would think so. I also worked with a local program last year called Presents for Patriots. I'd like to see if there's a way to expand the program this year," she said.

"Whoa," he said, lifting his hand and shaking his head. "I'm not the most jolly guy on the block these days. Maybe you'd better find someone who has more Christmas spirit."

Angie gaped at him in disbelief. "But everyone loves Christmas. It's the most wonderful time of the year."

Forrest blinked. *Was she serious?* She looked so crestfallen it was as if he'd told her that Santa didn't exist. He wondered if she was kidding, but quickly saw she wasn't. The woman was obviously over the moon about Christmas. Forrest had the feeling that refusing her would feel the same as kicking a puppy.

Mentally swearing, he sighed. "Okay, okay. I'll help."

She leaped toward him and put her arms around him. "Oh, thank you. I knew you'd be perfect."

Taken off guard by her impulsive embrace, Forrest tried not to notice how sweet her hair smelled within an inch of his nose and the way her breasts felt brushing against his chest. He glanced down at her pink lips and tried to remember the last time he'd kissed a woman.

At that forbidden thought, he quickly pulled back. "No one's ever accused me of being perfect."

Her gaze turned teasing. "Well, I can't imagine why."

That quick sexy glint in her eyes made him uneasy as hell. "Why don't you tell me some more about the Patriots program," he said, redirecting her attention, and hopefully his, too.

Angie gradually pulled back, but he would have

to be a dead man not to notice the way her hand skimmed over his knee or the fact that she didn't seem to mind sitting so close to him.

Forrest was torn. Was she so naive that she really didn't know what she was asking for? Or was she trying to seduce him?

Chapter Two

After her visit with Forrest, Angie felt as if she could have flown home. Surely, she wouldn't have needed her aging red Chevy pickup truck. Not after the way she'd teased a few grins from his serious mouth. She'd seen the way he'd stared at hers in curiosity. She just wished he'd given in to that emotion and kissed her.

She was in such a good mood when she pulled into the grocery store parking lot that she gave up a close space to another vehicle. She held the door for the elderly man behind her and returned his wink. As she wandered through the store, everything looked more vivid to her. The apples were redder, the grapes more purple. The oranges smelled delicious. Even the pork chops looked better than ever.

Angie picked up a few items and headed home. She couldn't wait to see Forrest again. Although she didn't enjoy housekeeping, she felt as if she needed to do something with her excess energy, so she ran the vacuum cleaner and cleaned the bathrooms. She was mopping the kitchen floor when a knock sounded at the side door.

Her brother, Austin, poked his head inside and his gaze fell to her mop. "What's the occasion? Are you having a party?"

Laughing, she shook her head. "No. I was just in the mood to clean, so I thought I'd better go with it."

"I'll say," he said, hitching his thumbs in his jean pockets. "From what I remember, the mood doesn't strike you very often at all."

Angie knew he was referring to how she'd often tried to get out of her chores during her teen years. "Oh, be quiet. I've been the main person to take care of cleaning since Haley left and you know it."

"Yeah, I guess," he relented. "What's got you in such a good mood? Sugar high? Cupcakes from the bakery?"

"No, but I'll have to say that Forrest is more delicious than a cupcake," she said and shot him a devilish smile.

"Forrest?" he said. "Forrest who?"

"Forrest Traub. He's an army veteran and he's staying in Thunder Canyon while his leg heals. I met him yesterday and, Austin, *he might be the one*."

"Whoa, whoa," Austin said, lifting his hand as he gingerly stepped across the drying kitchen floor. "You just met him yesterday and you already think he's the one? How can you know anything about him?"

"Look who's talking. It didn't take you long to fall for Rose."

"That's different. I'm older and more experienced," he said.

"I've been waiting for this feeling since I was born. I've had a sideline seat with a great view when Haley found love and then when you did, too. I want to belong to someone, also. I just never found the right someone, and, Austin, I really think he could be the one."

Austin touched her cheek. "Fairy girl," he said, calling her by the nickname he and Haley had used every now and then. "Don't rush into anything. You can't learn everything you need to know about a man in two sessions.

"And what about him?" Austin asked. "Does he feel the same way?"

"Oh, he's attracted to me," she said, laughing.

"How do you know that? Did he make a move on you?"

Angie rolled her eyes. "Of course not. He's not that kind. A woman just knows these things," she said.

Austin looked at her as if he thought she didn't have a clue. She had to bite her tongue to resist arguing with him further.

"I wouldn't be a decent brother if I didn't encourage you to take it slow. Even you have to admit that you've been known to lead with your heart instead of your head."

She nodded. "You've done your duty," she said. "Since you're here, do you mind checking out the truck? It's been making a funny noise lately." She didn't want any more of Austin's brotherly advice. Especially if he was going to discourage her about Forrest.

A few days later, Forrest's phone rang again, and this time he knew the caller's identification. Although he'd avoided officially adding Angie to his caller list, he knew her number. "Forrest Traub," he answered the phone.

"Angie Anderson," she mocked him in a deep voice. The giggle that followed ruined her stern tone.

He couldn't help grinning a little though he was glad she couldn't see. "How are you?"

"Wonderful. And you?" she asked.

"I wouldn't say wonderful, but not bad. What do you need?"

"Well, that's a wide-open question," she said in a husky voice that made his gut clench.

"I meant—"

"I know what you meant. I was hoping you and I could get together and talk some more about the projects we're planning. We don't have a lot of time before Christmas to get things going."

"True," he said. "What did you have in mind?"

"Well, I could bring over takeout tomorrow night," she suggested.

Forrest had a hard time turning down a meal. Although he could easily join his brother and Antonia at the main house, he couldn't help but feel he was intruding. "That would work. But this time, I pay."

"It's no big deal. Do you like Italian or Chinese?" she asked.

"Both when I don't have to prepare it," he said.

She chuckled. "Me, too. I'll surprise you, then. Tomorrow night around six?"

"Okay. See you then," he said and hung up the phone. Forrest couldn't help wondering what he was getting into by sharing another meal with Angie. He second-guessed himself, wondering if he should have kept their meeting in a public place. That way, neither of them would be tempted to do something they shouldn't. Not that he was all that tempted. Deep down, he knew that Angie was completely off-limits for him. She was a sweet, naive, young woman who had no clue just how dark his soul was. He had no intention of having her find out. In a strange way, he found her naivete precious, and he didn't want to destroy it.

The next night, Forrest ran the vacuum and did a little extra cleaning. He told himself it wasn't for Angie. It was because his suite needed it. Hell, it wasn't like he was lighting candles for her.

That thought soothed him at the same time he wondered if he should have gotten a bottle of wine. He'd been very careful with alcohol since he'd come back to the States. There was a high correlation between PTSD and alcoholism and drug abuse, and he was determined not to become a statistic. So far, he'd drank a beer every now and then, but that was all.

Rubbing his jaw, he wondered why he felt so edgy. In the scheme of things, Angie was just a kid.

A knock sounded at the door, pulling him out of his reverie. He felt an involuntary kick of excitement and scowled at himself. If he was getting this worked up over Angie, maybe he just needed to get out more often.

He opened the door and she grinned at him. "Hi there," she said holding a bag of what smelled like Chinese takeout in one hand and a tote full of papers in the other.

Forrest couldn't resist stealing an extra moment to take in the sight of her. Her unbuttoned red peacoat suited her bright personality, and the gray and white scarf around her neck tempted his gaze to fall into the V-neck of her gray sweater that gave a glimpse of her creamy cleavage. His mind followed his gaze and he couldn't help wondering...

Forrest jerked his gaze and thoughts away from Angie's breasts and he reached for the Chinese food. "Come on in. Smells good. What did you get?"

"Egg rolls, fried rice, kung pao chicken, sweet and sour pork, stir-fry beef with vegetables and of course fortune cookies. Will any of that work for you?"

Forrest felt his stomach growl. "All of it," he said. "I didn't realize how hungry I was."

"Well, I'm glad I could help out with that," she said and dumped her papers on the sofa and pulled off her coat. Feeling himself get distracted by her feminine shape again, Forrest deliberately headed for the kitchen. He began to pull out the boxes of food. "Whoa, this is enough for five soldiers," he said.

"I figured you might enjoy the leftovers," she said as she moved beside him. "I get the impression you don't enjoy cooking all that much."

"That's true. My brother keeps inviting me up to the house to eat with him and Antonia, but I feel like a fifth wheel. They're all goo-goo-eyed over each other, and with taking care of Clay's son and her baby, they've got enough to do."

"I don't mind cooking," she said. "But I don't really like cooking for one, so I either eat out or end up eating a lot of frozen dinners on the couch."

"It's mostly frozen dinners for me, too, so this is a treat," he said and put the boxes on a tray.

"Would you like some water?" she asked, pulling two glasses from the cabinet.

He nodded. "That works for me."

She filled the glasses and smiled at him. "I guess we're ready."

Forrest carefully carried the tray into the den and put it on the sofa table. He tore open his chopsticks and gave her a set. "Dig in," he said and started with the sweet and sour pork. "Good stuff," he said, making a mental note to visit the restaurant again. After a moment, he noticed Angie was looking at him and not eating.

He paused. "Problem?"

She blinked. "Uh, no," she said and tore the paper off her chopsticks. "I'm glad you like it." She reached for the container of kung pao chicken and gingerly arranged the chopsticks between her fingers. Plunging the wooden instruments into the food, she finally pulled up a bite of chicken. Victory flashed across her features as she lifted the bite to her mouth. And dropped it.

Forrest couldn't help chuckling. "I can get a fork for you," he offered.

"No, no. I've always thought I should learn how to do this, but I never got around to it," she said and tried to arrange her fingers around the chopsticks again.

Unable to resist helping her, Forrest set down his food and sticks. "Here," he said, repositioning her fingers. "Try that."

She successfully got a bite. "I did it," she said with pleasure that made something inside him feel warm. It took her a long time to get even a few more bites.

"You're doing good, but let me get you a fork. The food will be cold by the time you get to it."

She gave a mock pout. "And I thought I was doing so well."

"You were," he said as he rose. "You just need to practice when you're not hungry, so you can concentrate better."

"When did you get so handy with those sticks?" she asked

Forrest grabbed a fork from the kitchen and returned. "I've been stationed in a lot of places, and most of them have Chinese restaurants." He picked up the sticks and clicked them together.

"That sweet and sour pork looks pretty good," she said.

He picked up a bite with the chopsticks and held

it out to her mouth. Her lips opened and she took a bite, closing her eyes. "Yum." The expression on her face made his mind wonder how her mouth would feel against his. He couldn't help wondering if she would be as enthusiastic in bed. He cleared his throat hoping it would also clear his mind.

"So what do you want to do next for the charity plans?"

She nodded. "Good question. Along with the holiday cards and letters, I may be able to get some small donations for gifts for the soldiers. Do you have any suggestions?"

"Phone cards and gift cards," he said then grinned in memory. "But well-packed cookies are rarely refused."

"Making the cookies would be a fun project. I'll have to consult you on the packing."

"I can do that," he said.

"I love baking Christmas cookies. When I was a teenager, I sometimes talked my brother and sister into baking them with me in the summer. They thought I was crazy, but everyone enjoyed the results."

Forrest was curious, again, about Angie's parents. "Bet you were a cute kid. They indulged you."

She shrugged. "My mom died in a car accident. Before that, my dad left just after I was born. My brother and sister tried to make up for my missing out on having a mom and dad."

He nodded. "Sounds rough."

"Sometimes," she admitted. "But it could have been lots worse. We had a roof over our head. Due to my mom's life insurance, the house was paid for. Sometimes, I feel guilty for how much my sister and brother sacrificed, but then they tell me that I helped them keep centered. They said that taking care of me helped them with their own pain."

"But you're not sure," he said, sensing her uncertainty.

She bit her lip. "Guess not."

He couldn't help a half smile. "I'm betting you brought a lot of magic to them. You gave them smiles and happiness, but you didn't know it at the time."

"Think so?" she asked doubtfully.

He nodded. "Yeah."

Angie stared at him for a long intense moment. "I hadn't thought about that."

"Everyone has a role," he said.

"Did you learn that in the army?" she asked.

"I did."

"I'll have to think that over," she said and her lips tilted in a sexy smile.

That smile distracted him enough that he didn't feel hungry anymore. At least, not for food. He swallowed over a tight lump of desire in his throat. "What else do you have in mind for the letters-for-soldiers plan?"

"Just what I told you," she said. "I like your idea of cookies. I can bake an extra dozen for you," she offered.

His gut twisted at her sensual expression. He shouldn't be feeling this way. Yet, he couldn't force himself to step back from her. "Not necessary," he managed, but he knew his tone wasn't forceful.

"Necessary isn't always the bottom line," she said, holding his gaze.

He sucked in a quick breath and told himself to pull away.

She leaned toward him, and he couldn't resist the need to feel her closer. It was primal. It rolled from deep inside him.

She drew closer and closer until her lips were a millimeter from his.

Forrest inhaled her scent. Three times. Nothing was enough. She was a mix of innocence, excitement and sensuality. And he wanted her.

Agonizing seconds passed. She pressed her mouth against his.

Forrest felt a shot of electricity race through him, and he wanted more. She was everything he'd wanted, but hadn't had for what felt like ages. Her scent surrounded him like a delicious veil, her breath enveloped his and some sort of foreign emotion ricocheted through him.

Unable to resist her, he slid his fingers through her hair. She kissed him again, and the soft pucker of her lips made him hungrier than ever. He groaned and she slid her tongue over his. The sensual gesture sent him over the top and he took her lips in a sexual, bonding kiss. He wanted her mouth. He wanted all of her.

Forrest pulled her against him and devoured her with his mouth. She tasted delicious, sensual, irresistible. He felt his control waiver. He wanted to take her to bed and get her naked then slide inside her and …

No, he told himself. It would be wrong. She was innocent. She had no idea what she would be getting into.

Forrest forced himself to let go. His heart was pounding and he fought to catch his breath.

Angie's breath lifted her chest, distracting the devil out of him at the same time that her gorgeous lips puckered in invitation. Forrest was learning a new level of hell.

"Why'd you stop?" she asked.

His gut twisted in arousal. "Because," he said. "Because it was wrong."

Her eyebrows furrowed in confusion. "Wrong? It felt pretty right to me."

He clenched his jaw. "Trust me. We shouldn't have done that."

Angie frowned. "Are you saying you didn't want to kiss me?"

His gut twisted into a square knot. "I didn't say that," he muttered. "That's not the point."

"Why isn't it?" she asked. "If I want you and you want me—"

"It could be a big mess," he said and stood, feeling out of control. "What else do we need to cover for the charity stuff?"

Feeling her gaze on him, he picked up the rest of the Chinese food and took it to the kitchen. "Do you want to take any of this home?" he called from the kitchen.

"No," she said. "I'm good."

Forrest shoved the leftovers into his fridge and took a deep breath. Why had he gone after her like that? It made him feel like some kind of sexual madman. He took another deep breath, determined to take responsibility. Returning to the den, he steeled himself before he met her gaze.

She rose to face him. His gut tightened and he thought about all the reasons he shouldn't be attracted to her. She leaned toward him.

"This isn't a good idea," he muttered.

"I think it's a great idea," she said and smiled her wicked, innocent, sexy smile.

He clenched his jaw again. "That's because you don't know better," he told her. "I'm too old for you."

"Too old?" she echoed. "That's crazy. How old are you?"

"Thirty-one, but in terms of experience—"

Angie rolled her eyes. "You exaggerated. You're just finding your feet and your way. That's why you feel unsure."

"I don't know about that," Forrest said.

"Well, I do," she said in a husky whisper as she leaned toward him.

"You need to leave," he said.

"Isn't that a bit drastic?" she asked.

"Not at all," he said and steeled himself not to respond to her.

"Just one more kiss," she whispered in an inviting voice.

"No," he said, but it killed him.

Later that night, Forrest settled into his bed, but his mind continued to race. He needed to be more careful about Angie. She was more impulsive than he was. She clearly wanted him and had no interest in waiting. That meant trouble. She was making herself completely available to him.

How the hell was he supposed to resist that?

Forrest took another deep breath as he rested his head on his pillow. He needed some of that Zen stuff.

He did *not* want to be fighting his sexual needs with Angie. Step back, he told himself. In every emotional and physical way, he had to walk away.

Since he was clearly more mature than she was, he would have to take the high road. Even though he found her far more tempting than he should. And now he would have the memory of that kiss they'd shared. Swearing under his breath, he turned on his side and closed his eyes. But the image of Angie's sexy mouth taunted him.

It seemed to take hours, but Forrest finally fell asleep. When he awakened in the morning, he felt a sense of anticipation. He hadn't had that in a long time. Today he was holding the first meeting of the war veterans support group. Part of him wondered if anyone would show up. He'd included a photo of Smiley in the flyers and website announcement for the group. He supposed if nothing else, some of the veterans might show up for some free food. A local deli was donating sandwiches and cookies for the first meeting.

Swinging his legs over the edge of the bed, he sat up and stretched his bad leg, willing it to get stronger. Forrest knew he would be struggling with his injury for the rest of his life, so there was no room for feeling sorry for himself. Rising from the bed, he headed toward his workout equipment. He might have a bum leg, but he was damned if the rest of him wouldn't be as strong as possible.

A few hours later, Forrest arrived at the hospital conference room early with the sandwiches and cookies, and set the chairs in a circle. Annabel Cates rushed into the room with Smiley on a leash.

"Here he is," she said. "Ready to work his canine magic. Plus a few treats you can give him," she added, handing him a plastic bag.

Forrest's heart lifted at the sight of the dog. "Good to see you, Smiley," he said and rubbed the dog behind his ears. Smiley thumped his tail in response.

"He should be on his best behavior since I gave him some retraining. Can't let him forget the rules. If you need me for anything, give me a call," she said. "You've got my cell, right?"

"I've got it and thank you for loaning him to us," Forrest said. "I think he'll help break the ice."

"This is a good thing you're doing, Forrest. I'm glad if Smiley can help in any way. Just don't give him any of those sandwiches," she warned him. "No matter how sweet he looks, we've got to keep him disciplined if he's going to be helpful."

"Yes, ma'am," he said. "You're the one giving the orders."

Annabel gave a quick nod with a smile. "I'll see you afterward. Have fun," she said and darted out the door.

"Fun," Forrest echoed. That was one word he wouldn't have associated with a support group. He shrugged and looked at Smiley. "Maybe she knows something I don't."

Less that two minutes later, a man wearing a ball-cap and an open down jacket walked through the door. "Is this the war veterans support group?"

"It sure is," Forrest said. "I'm Forrest Traub, army."

The man nodded. "Iraq?" he said.

Forrest nodded. "And you?"

"Afghanistan. Steve Henderson. I've been back almost eighteen months."

Smiley walked toward the man and looked at him, thumping his tail in welcome.

Steve bent down to pet the dog and gave a half grin. "Is this our mascot?"

"Yep, that's Smiley. He's a therapy dog on loan to us, and I'll vouch for him. He'll always be glad to see you," Forrest said.

"Well, that's a lot more than we can say about most humans," Steve said.

Just then, another man walked through the door, then another. Smiley greeted each one, and Forrest could practically see a bit of tension ease out of the men at the sight of the dog. Eyeing the clock, he sensed that he should start the meeting and closed the door.

"Welcome, everyone. I hope you enjoyed the sandwiches and Smiley."

The men took their seats and murmured in agreement.

"The first thing I want to tell you is that you don't have to talk if you don't want to. I have to be honest. Most of the time, I would rather do anything than talk about what I saw and experienced in Iraq."

Several of the men nodded.

"But since this group was my idea, I guess I've got to go first."

A few chuckles rippled through the small group.

Forrest took a deep breath. "During my last two tours, all I could think about was the day I would finally come home. I was determined to be career military, but seeing all those guys get hurt was tough. Being in Iraq was surreal, and not in a good way. Once I got home, though, it was Montana that didn't seem like the real world anymore. People couldn't understand what I'd been through, what I'd seen. And I got tired of explaining it."

"So what helps?" one of the vets asked.

Forrest shrugged. "I don't have all the answers. I have to admit, I took the coward's way out—leaving home. After being home, I had to get out. I just moved to Thunder Canyon a few months ago. Folks don't know me here as well since my brother and I haven't lived here very long. They don't have any expectations." He paused. "What helps? Smiley sure does." The dog licked him and laughter rippled through the small room.

The laughter turned to silence. "The nights are the worst. I'm back there, and the shells are flying, and I can't stop screaming," Steve offered. A few of the others nodded in agreement.

"The nightmares are bad. They feel so real," Forrest said.

"Coming back to my wife helped me," one of the men said. "She's the reason I keep going."

"I felt that way about my girlfriend," another soldier said. "But it's hard now. I'm not the same man I was before. I'm not sure it's going to work out. What about you, Forrest? Do you have anyone special in your life?"

An image of Angie flashed in his mind, taking him by surprise. He shook his head for his own benefit as much as the others. "No. I'm not ready for a relationship. I'm busy putting Humpty Dumpty back together. That doesn't mean you guys aren't ready, though," he quickly added. "We're all at different places in this. It's not easy. That's why I wanted to start this group." He glanced at the clock. "Hard to believe, but our time is up."

He gave a wry grin. "And we all survived."

Chapter Three

After Annabel picked up Smiley, Forrest headed home, his mind swimming with the stories the men in the group had shared. Most of them had said they would return. That made Forrest feel good about starting the group and putting himself out there. Lord knew, he was the last man to want to expose himself to anyone, let alone a group of strangers. That said, even though he'd never met any of the men who'd attended the meeting before, he'd felt an immediate connection with them.

He pulled into the driveway to his current home. Driving toward the boardinghouse, he spotted his brother outside the main house. He waved and slowed as Clay lifted his hand. Forrest lowered his window. "Hey, how's it going?"

"I could ask you the same question, stranger," Clay said. "You haven't been by for breakfast in over a week."

Forrest shrugged. "Hate to interrupt the lovefest," he said and shot his brother a half grin.

"Yeah, yeah. That excuse doesn't wash with me. Why don't you come in for some coffee?" Clay asked. "Or soda.... Or something? Antonia made some great pastries this morning," he added in a tempting voice.

Forrest wasn't the least bit hungry, but he'd missed his brother. "Okay, you twisted my arm. Where is your woman and the babies?"

"She's gone to town for her post-baby checkup with the doctor and took the baby with her. Bennett is inside taking a nap," Clay said and lifted a nursery monitor. "But I'm never far away."

Forrest nodded, raised his window and pulled his car to the main house. He stepped outside and felt his leg dip. Cursing the weakness, he leaned more heavily on his other leg. He knew, however, that he couldn't do that on a regular basis because his whole body, including his spine and neck would eventually feel the strain of it. That was why he needed to continue his strength conditioning.

He strode slowly up the steps to the porch. Clay

skipped past him to the door and pushed it open. For a sliver of a second, Forrest couldn't help envying his brother's agility. Pushing it aside, Forrest followed his brother inside toward Antonia's kitchen where he'd consumed many hearty breakfasts with her, his brother and his nephew Bennett.

Clay reached for the coffeemaker and poured two cups. "Here ya go," he said, handing one to Forrest.

"Thanks," Forrest said and followed Clay to sit at the kitchen table.

"So, what's up with you?" Clay asked. "Did you have a doctor visit today?"

Forrest shook his head. "Not today. I started a support group for veterans at the hospital. I'm even using a therapy support dog."

Clay blinked. "You're kidding."

Forrest shook his head. "Nope. It went pretty well. Gotta tell you I think the free sandwiches and Smiley made a big difference."

"Smiley?" Clay asked.

"Yeah, he's the therapy dog. He belongs to Annabel Cates. He's a real sweetheart. The best icebreaker ever."

"Cool. So you're glad about how it went?" Clay asked.

"Yeah, I am. On the other hand, I've been roped into working with the ROOTS group to—"

"ROOTS?" Clay echoed.

"It's some kind of youth program," Forrest said. "First, they wanted my assistance with a G.I. Christmas card project, and now they're asking me to help with some kind of holiday celebration for local military families."

Clay frowned. "How'd you get dragged into that?"

"It's kinda weird," Forrest said and took a sip of black coffee. "I was walking Smiley, the therapy dog, and he got away from me. He went to ROOTS and this girl named Angie was there."

Clay lifted his brows. "A girl?"

"Yeah."

Clay sipped his coffee. "What's this Angie like?"

"Young," Forrest said. "Naive. Pretty," he said grudgingly. "Affectionate."

Clay's mouth formed an O of surprise. "Affectionate. What'd she do? Kiss you?"

Forrest clenched his jaw and took a shallow breath. "Maybe."

Silence followed then Clay chuckled. "Woot. Good for you."

Forrest scowled. "Or not. This girl is trouble. She's way too young for me."

Clay immediately turned solemn. "What do you mean? Is she under eighteen?"

"Hell, no. I'm not that stupid," Forrest said. "She's twenty-three."

Clay waved his hand in dismissal. "That's not too

young. Last I heard, twenty-three is past the age of consent."

"You're not getting my point," Forrest said. "She's young, innocent, happy. I'm old, fighting a bum leg and plagued by nightmares."

"You're scared," Clay said, his eyes rounding in astonishment. "My big bad brother who faced the enemy overseas is being taken down by a *girl*."

Forrest scowled again. "That's the problem. She looks at me like a G.I. Joe doll. I would never be able to live up to her expectations. Plus I'm just too old for her."

"Why don't you chill out? Hell, it's not like you're Methuselah. You can't get senior-citizen discounts yet. There's no crime in seeing where this goes. She sounds nice."

"Hmm," Forrest says, studying his brother. He couldn't quite get used to the change in Clay since he and Antonia had gotten engaged. "You sure have changed your tune lately. Mr. I'm-Not-Going-To-Get-Involved is now the King of Romance?"

"A little romance might be good for you," Clay said. "Might put an extra spring in the step of that ornery leg of yours. For that matter, it might make you a little less ornery period."

"And Merry Christmas to you, too," Forrest said in dry tone.

"You better be getting your jolly on. It looks like

you're going to be busy this Christmas. Ho, ho, bro," Clay said and laughed, clearly amused at his own joke.

After arranging for extra coverage at ROOTS, Angie prepared to join those scheduled to go to the animal shelter. She and Jennifer, the regular volunteer who headed this group, rounded up the kids. A couple minutes before they planned to leave, a red-haired teen walked in the door. He looked around uncertainly.

"I think that's Joey, Lilly's brother," Angie said to Jennifer. "Do you want to go talk to him?"

"Sure," Jennifer said. Jennifer was a middle-aged woman who devoted many hours to ROOTS after her own children had suffered some troubles during their teenage years. Now that her kids were graduating from college, she had some extra time on her hands and especially enjoyed the ROOTS visits at the animal shelter.

Angie was thrilled that Joey had decided to join them. From her peripheral vision she glimpsed the door to the center opening again. She immediately knew the identity of the man. *Forrest.* Her heart skipped over itself and she struggled with mixed emotions, holding herself in check. Even though she had felt crushed when he'd rejected her, she still felt excited to see him.

He walked toward her.

"Hi," she said. "What a nice surprise to see you."

He nodded. "I remembered you said something about working at ROOTS on Thursday afternoons, so I thought we could knock out more holiday plans."

Disappointment swept through her. "I wish I could, but I'm committed to go with the animal shelter team. One of the other teens has been worried about her brother, so I thought it would be a good idea to observe him today." She paused for a moment. "I would love it if you would come, and it would be so great for the teens to see a man willing to donate some time to an animal shelter."

He opened his mouth and based on his expression, Angie expected him to refuse. "But no pressure. You probably have other things you can do."

He closed his mouth and sighed with a half chuckle. "Not at this exact moment. What's on tap with the animals tonight?"

Angie resisted the urge to clap in delight. "Whatever the people at the shelter ask us to do. Everything from cleaning cages and doing laundry to taking dogs for a walk or just giving the animals some extra attention. Do you mind if I introduce you to the kids after we get there? I think it will give them an extra boost knowing a veteran is joining us."

"Or they might just think I'm some old dude with a limp."

She frowned at his remark. "No one could ever think that about you. Ever," she said.

He looked away as if he suddenly felt self-conscious. "If you think it'll make a difference, then go for it," he said.

Everyone except Forrest piled into the van. Angie suspected he was more comfortable in his own vehicle. She halfway wondered if he would change his mind before they all arrived at the shelter, but he pulled in right behind the van.

As the kids exited, she waved them toward her. "Just a quick announcement. We have a special guest tonight. Major Forrest Traub, an army veteran. Make him feel welcome."

The kids gave a chorus of hellos and Forrest smiled and nodded. The group entered the building and a shelter employee met them. "Thank you for coming," the young woman said. "We have a lot of animals, so we need a lot of help. I need volunteers to clean kennels, walk dogs and play with cats and kittens."

She noticed that Forrest immediately volunteered to clean the cages. Most people would rather handle animals. Angie was designated a floater and used the time to observe Lilly's brother, Joey. He seemed to love handling the kittens.

She sidled next to him. "Hi, I'm Angie," she said.

"I'm Joey," he said, but kept petting the kittens.

"Did the shelter person tell you why the kittens need to be handled?" she asked, reaching over to cuddle one of the furry creatures.

He nodded. "So they'll be tame with humans. If they're not touched regularly, then they'll go wild."

"Looks like you're pretty good at it," she said.

"I like animals," he said. "Animals won't hurt you if you treat them right. You can't always count on that with humans."

"Hmm," she said. "I'm glad you came tonight."

He glanced up and met her gaze. "I am, too."

"Then I hope you'll come back," she said. "I need to check on the guy cleaning the kennels."

"He took the dirty job," Joey said.

"Yeah, I think he's probably done that more than once," she said, thinking about the assignments Forrest may have been given throughout his military career. The fact that he didn't shirk doing the hard stuff made him all the more attractive to her.

Asking directions, she walked to the back of the facility to a room with several drains in the floor. She hugged her arms around herself as she saw him, dressed in a jumpsuit and boots provided by the shelter, spraying the kennels. "Kinda chilly back here," she said.

He turned to look at her and nodded. "Could be worse. I like that it just takes a little time for them to have a clean bed. After my first three surgeries, they offered me a chance to work with animals at a no-kill shelter. It's surprising what a difference pets can make in physical and mental recovery."

"Do you think you'd like to have a dog?" she asked.

He tossed a glance at her. "I get to borrow Smiley right now," he said. "I'm in line for another surgery or two. Maybe after that."

He turned back to his task and she stared at his strong solitary figure. She wondered if he would ever decide he didn't want to be so alone. He was determined, used to fending for himself, but something inside her sensed he could want her enough to open up. Angie sighed. It might take awhile.

After the group returned to the ROOTS building, Angie was surprised when Forrest came inside. "Hey," she said. "I thought we might have worn you out."

"I'm good. I wondered if you want to talk about the ROOTS for Soldiers pen pal program."

"Sure," she said, pleased. "How about if we hit the diner for some coffee or hot chocolate? We could grab a sandwich if you're hungry," she suggested.

He shot her a hesitant, wary glance, and Angie knew he was thinking about the way she'd jumped him. "Hey, I don't bite," she said with a chuckle. "Unless I'm asked and never in public."

He gave an uncomfortable-sounding laugh. "Okay,"

he said. "I'm a little hungry. We can kill two birds with one stone."

"Okay, let me say my goodbyes," she said and made sure she talked to each teen, including Joey.

After she finished, she met him at the door and pushed her hands in her pockets. "Ready."

He nodded and opened the door. The brisk air hit them in the face.

"Nothing like Montana in November," she said. "Or January or February,"

"Better than Iraq anytime," he said, shoving his hands into his pockets. "It got up to 138 degrees during one of my tours."

"138?" she echoed, gaping at him. "That's horrible."

"Gives new meaning to *hell on earth,*" he said with a dry chuckle. "We fried an egg on the top of a Humvee."

"If you hated it, why didn't you just quit?" she asked. "I mean, at the end of your tour or whatever."

"It was what I was supposed to do. I never doubted it. It felt right even when it felt like crap," he said.

"Even when you did the dirty work," she murmured.

He glanced at her and held her gaze for a long moment. "Yeah, I guess."

"Told you that you're a hero," she said.

He rolled his eyes. "I'm no G.I. Joe doll," he said.

"You look pretty darn good to me," she said and saw him tilt his head in warning. "But we're going to talk about the ROOTS for Soldiers program. And the diner is calling us," she said pointing to the building down the block.

"True," he said and held open the door for her as they entered the cozy place.

The waitress waved them toward an empty booth.

"I love this place," she said, pulling her scarf from around her neck and unbuttoning her coat. "They make the best grilled cheese sandwiches in the world."

"Is that what you're going to order?"

"Absolutely. And hot chocolate loaded with marshmallows. I want my sugar high," she said, grinning at him as she sat across from him in a red booth. "Are you going to order something sensible?"

"I don't know. I may order meat loaf and pie," he said.

"Oooh," she said, shaking her finger at him. "Bad boy."

He laughed. "I'll pay for it, but their pie is worth it."

"It is," she said.

The waitress delivered menus and ice water.

"So what's the next step with the ROOTS for Soldiers program?" he asked.

"I'd like to set up a couple times for you to talk to

the kids. The reason I would like you to speak more than once is because not all the kids come each time. I'd like to choose the peak times," she said.

"What do you want me to tell them?" he asked, his hands forming a tent as he leaned toward her.

His intensity just got to her. She felt her belly do a crazy little dance and looked away from him to hide it. "I just want you to talk about what it was like to be there. To get mail from people you didn't know. How much it meant to you." She glanced up again. "Did you ever spend the holidays in Iraq?"

He nodded. "Many times. It was hard," he confessed. "It felt like the rest of the world was celebrating without us."

"I know that feeling," she said, the feeling of loss from years ago echoing inside her. "Right after my mom died, the last thing I wanted to do was celebrate the holidays. Everyone else seemed so happy, but all I could think about was what was missing."

Forrest met her gaze. "What changed? You're all about Christmas now. Sheesh, you could be Santa's elf."

She smiled. "I don't know when it happened, but eventually I realized that the best way to honor my mom was by remembering the good times. My mom had always loved Christmas and so had I. Celebrating Christmas is a way I can keep her close to me. Plus there was the matter of my brother and my sister. They tried desperately to make the holidays special, and I think my excitement helped them with their grief. Strange how it all ties together, isn't it?" she asked.

"I never thought about it from that perspective. It's similar to folks wishing their soldiers were home with them," he murmured. "It must be hard for the families at home to keep up their spirits."

The waitress arrived to take their orders.

Angie took a deep breath and the silence between them felt companionable, connected. She didn't feel the sudden need to fill it with idle conversation. What a novel experience for her, she thought, savoring the moment.

The waitress delivered their hot chocolate.

"I wonder if there's something that could be done for the families," he mused.

"That's a great idea," Angie said, her mind spinning with ideas. "I'm glad we're doing the ROOTS for Soldiers program, but we could try to do something for the families of GIs who can't be home. Maybe a meal or something. Thanksgiving or Christmas Eve?"

He nodded. "Hey, maybe DJ could help. He *is* my cousin and he runs the Rib Shack."

"And did you know he gave turkeys to people who otherwise wouldn't have a hot meal last year? He's always been generous with the community," she said.

"So, maybe the Rib Shack could hold a party for military families," he suggested as the waitress delivered their meal.

Angie moved her head from side to side in half agreement. "Maybe," she said.

"Maybe?" he said, wrinkling his eyebrows in confusion.

"The Rib Shack would be very nice," she said, her mind brimming with other ideas. "But wouldn't it be even nicer if the families could be treated like royalty?"

"Does this mean we'll be contacting Buckingham Palace?" he asked in a wry voice as he dug into his meat loaf and mashed potatoes.

Angie laughed. "I was thinking of something a little closer to home. Say, dinner at the Gallatin Room."

Forrest nearly choked on his meat loaf. He coughed and swallowed hard. "The Gallatin Room. Can't say I've been there, but I've heard it's the fanciest place in Thunder Canyon. What makes you think Thunder Canyon Resort would be interested in this kind of gig?"

"You never know until you ask," she said. "I'm going to talk to Grant Clifton. He's the manager of the resort. I'll see what he can do," she said and took a bite of her grilled cheese sandwich.

"I guess this means Grant's going to be holding a

Thanksgiving dinner for families of soldiers," Forrest said.

"I'm hopeful," she said. "But what makes you so sure?"

"You seem to know how to get people to do what you want them to do," he said as he continued to eat. "I'm trying to remember when I met someone better at twisting arms than you."

"You could have said no," she told him.

"Yeah, if I'd wanted to end up with coal in my stocking. Once you started in about how wonderful Christmas is, I would have felt like I was kicking a puppy if I'd turned you down."

"So, you're saying your decision to help me was based on pity," she said, putting as much indignation into her voice as possible.

"Well, part of it," he admitted with a cautious expression on his face.

"Okay," she said, smiling at him. "I'll remember that for next time."

Forrest groaned. "Help," he said in a croaky voice.

Angie couldn't help laughing. Forrest was such a strong man, all man, as she knew from getting so close to him during that kiss they'd shared. "How could a woman like me scare a soldier like you?"

He looked at her with a perplexed expression on his face. "I can't explain it. Maybe you have some secret superpowers you haven't told me about."

Angie met his gaze. *Was he flirting with her?* She quickly denied the possibility. Not Forrest. He was still holding her at arm's length. She would have to lure him in, and it wasn't going to be easy.

A couple days later, after a little more arm-twisting, Forrest joined Angie for her visit with Grant Clifton. "We have a fantastic idea," she said to Grant as they sat in his office.

Grant leaned back in his chair and folded his hands. "Tell me about it," he said. *Sell me,* his body language said.

"Major Forrest Traub and I have found an unmet need in our community. We've begun a program where the ROOTS teens are corresponding with soldiers out of the country, sending them letters and small gifts. What Forrest and I realized is that we haven't addressed the stateside families of soldiers who can't come home for the holidays. There's no way we can compensate for that, but that doesn't mean we shouldn't try," she said.

Grant grinned. "Okay, what's your idea?"

"We want the families to feel like royalty. We want them to have the chance to dine in the Gallatin Room on Thanksgiving Day Eve."

Silence followed, and Angie resisted the urge to grab Forrest's hand. He'd endured her hours of practice before this meeting and reluctantly agreed to join her.

Grant leaned forward and drummed his fingers on his desk. "That's actually not a bad idea," he finally said. "Thanksgiving is a big day for us, but the night before Thanksgiving isn't that big. We could give you a lot of attention that night. We could give you the attention you deserve."

Angie slumped in relief. "Really?"

Grant nodded. "Really," he said. "It doesn't hurt that you brought a soldier with you."

Forrest lifted his hand. "Didn't say a word."

"You didn't have to," Grant said with a solemn face. "Thank you for your service and sacrifice."

Surprised by the man's words, Forrest nodded. "Thank you, but I was just doing my job."

"Then, thank you for doing your job. It's a helluva lot more hazardous than mine is," Grant said.

Forrest grinned. "I dunno. If you put me in the kitchen, it could get dangerous."

Grant laughed. "Then we won't let you near it," he said, turning to Angie. "We can work out a menu with our new chef. I'm sure he will be more than willing to participate."

Angie jumped to her feet. "This is fabulous. Thank you so much."

Forrest rose beside her. "The veterans thank you," he said. "The community thanks you."

"Nothing I can do will match what you've given for our country," Grant said and lifted his hand. "No debates please." He extended his hand to Forrest.

Forrest strongly clasped the man's hand and nodded.

"We'll be in touch," Angie said and gave a little salute.

She walked out the door of the manager's office and she grabbed Forrest's hand. They walked down a hall, a set of stairs and another hall. When they stepped outside, she squealed at the top of her lungs.

"We did it!"

He laughed. "You did," he corrected, enjoying her exuberance.

"With your help," she said, jumping up and down.

"I just sat there," he said. "You did the persuading. You used your superpowers."

"Yeah, right," she said. "You made a huge difference. Don't argue with me. Thank you for coming."

"It wasn't a tough job. Like I said, all I had to do was sit there," he said.

"And be yourself. Being yourself is pretty awesome," she said.

He shrugged, thinking about how much he still needed to accomplish to gain back his former self. "I'm working at it."

"Well, can I buy you a cup of hot chocolate?" she asked, tilting her head to the side.

She made it hard for him to refuse. "I'll take a rain check," he said. "No sugar for me. I want to sleep tonight."

"No problem," she said as they walked to his truck. "Do you have a hard time sleeping at night?"

He felt his gut twist. "Depends on the night. I have some leftovers from the war."

She looked at him. "That makes perfect sense," she said. "Anyone who experienced the kind of trauma you did would have a hard time sometimes."

He felt an easing inside him. How could she begin to know what he'd been through? Yet, her words felt like cool water over an aching wound.

Forrest helped her into the passenger seat of his truck and rounded the vehicle to the driver's side. He got inside, pulled on his safety belt and started the car. Driving to her home, he thought about how much Angie contributed to the community. She looked like a cute flighty fairy, but he was learning that she was far more than that.

He pulled his truck to a stop and turned to her. "You did a good thing tonight," he said. "Thanks."

Her eyes widened in surprise. "Thanks to you. You inspired me."

Everything inside him wanted to pull her to him and take her lips in a kiss. But he resisted. He had to. He sighed and nodded. "I'll see you soon."

Chapter Four

The next night, Forrest gave a brief presentation to the ROOTS group.

"The desert in Iraq is cruel. It can reach temperatures of 138 degrees Fahrenheit in the summer and below freezing in winter. Some of us saw snow, but not sleigh-riding snow. And there are no Christmas lights or Christmas trees in Iraq unless we keep them undercover. We don't want to call attention to ourselves." Forrest took a breath. "The great thing is you can do something to help. Your cards and letters, cookies and small gifts, make us feel like we're not all alone."

One of the ROOTS teens raised his hand. "How can a card from me make a difference?"

"It's like a vacation away from Iraq. Especially if you tell us what you're doing, or even what you want to be doing. Your letter takes us away from where we are for just a few minutes. And sometimes that's all we need," Forrest said.

"But are the cookies we send to you stale by the time you receive them?" a girl asked.

Forrest shook his head. "No, but even if they were, we'd eat them all. There's nothing like cookies from home."

The girl smiled.

"Did you ever worry about dying?" a male teen asked.

Forrest sat back in his chair, wanting to give the best answer. "I wouldn't say we worry about that because we didn't have enough time. But the possibility was always there. And we always had to be ready."

"And what about when you got injured?" the same teen asked.

Angie stood. "I think that's enough for tonight. We don't want to wear out our guest—"

Forrest lifted his hand. "It's okay. I can take this. I never planned for this injury. I thought about the possibility of death, but not this, so I've got a different battle now. It's not easy. Hey, I bet your life isn't always easy."

The youths muttered in response.

"So, I'm just doing the best I can. I'm lucky to have people around me who want to help me succeed. You're in the same situation. You've got people around you who want you to succeed, so you know what I'm talking about."

Silence followed, then the teens began to applaud. The applause grew to a roar and Forrest met Angie's gaze. He hadn't been crazy about giving this talk, but now he knew it had been necessary. It was good for the ROOTS teens to see that he was struggling. It made them feel less alone. And hopefully inspired.

Thank you, Angie mouthed to him.

She stood. "If you want to get involved in ROOTS for Soldiers, you can sign up at the table on the other side of the room. We will also be sending long-distance phone cards and we need elfs to help bake cookies for soldiers."

A couple of the kids came toward him. "Thanks for coming, Major Traub. I'm sorry you got hurt," a teen girl said.

Forrest shrugged. "I came out alive. I just need to make the best of it."

The teen girl leaned toward him. "Well, you look really buff for an older guy," she whispered.

Forrest was both flattered and amused. "Thanks," he said. "I work at it."

A teen guy frowned at the girl. "What'd you say to him? Were you flirting with him?" he asked.

"Pity compliment," Forrest quickly said, pointing to his leg. "My injury."

The guy nodded. "Sorry," he said and lifted his hand for a fist bump. "You're the man," he said.

Moments later, he felt Angie at his side. "Sorry if that was a little rough," she said.

"Not rough at all," Forrest said. "Nothing close to what I would have expected during an interrogation. No one says you're buff during an interrogation."

Angie lifted her eyebrows in surprise. "Who said that?"

"One of your girls," he said, crossing his arms over his chest.

"Well, hello, I already told you that," she said. "And I'm past puberty."

He jerked his head to meet her gaze. "You wouldn't know that by looking at you."

"Well, maybe your vision isn't too good, old man," she teased him, sending him a sly, sideways glance.

He gave a low growl.

She smiled at him. "I like that. You want some hot chocolate at the diner?"

"Light on the marshmallows," he said.

Angie sighed. "One of these days you're not going to be able to resist me," she said. "I'm going to persuade you to dump a ton of marshmallows in your hot chocolate."

His gut twisted. She wasn't seducing him or pushing herself on him. In fact, she had barely touched him lately, and he told himself that was a good thing. He had no business even thinking about touching her or kissing her let alone actually doing it. When he was around Angie, though, his temperature seemed to rise on its own, and his mind wandered to that kiss they'd shared and how she'd felt in his arms. Somehow he always managed to pull himself under control. Thank God for his self-discipline. Otherwise, he would have to avoid her, and Forrest was reluctant to deprive himself of her presence. Despite his pain and gloominess, being around her just made him feel better.

They walked to the diner and got the "usual."

"Well, Miss Christmas, have you decorated your house yet?" Forrest asked Angie as they sipped their hot chocolate.

"No, I'm behind this year because of the ROOTS projects and my college courses. I'm only taking two, but both require a paper, and I've learned the sad truth that they won't write themselves. Darn it," she said with a soft chuckle.

"Do you know what you want to do when you finish your degree?"

Angie winced. "I could probably graduate with a general degree next spring. With this particular degree, I would be qualified to ask, 'Do you want fries with that?'

"Oh, come on. It can't be that bad. You have experience in a lot of things," he said.

"Yes, but I'm doing most of them for free or for very low wages. I'll figure it out," she said with a shrug. "I usually do."

"You're very good with the ROOTS kids. Would you want to work full-time with them?" he asked.

"I would, but ROOTS doesn't take on a lot of full-time workers. I might have to go somewhere else." She glanced down into her cup. "I'm not ready for that."

"That's okay," he said in a low voice and slid his hand over hers.

Angie looked up and met his gaze. "Thank you for saying that."

He nodded slowly. "You've made a huge impact on those kids, and you continue to do that."

She took a deep breath. "Thanks—" She broke off when her cell phone rang. "I should ignore it," she said then frowned. "But, I can't." She dug in her purse. "Angie here," she said into the phone.

Forrest watched as her eyes widened. A gap of silence followed and Angie's brow furrowed in concern. "I'll be right over, Lilly. Thank you for calling me." She turned off her phone. "I have to go. Lilly's brother Joey was beat up after school."

Forrest's gut clenched as he remembered the skinny kid who had clearly loved animals. "I'll go with you," he said, shoving aside his hot chocolate. He was no longer hungry.

"Are you sure? Between Lilly and her mother, there might be a bit of emotion," she said.

"I can handle it," he said. "I'll follow you in my truck."

Less than a half hour later, Forrest joined Angie as she entered Lilly's house. Lilly was crying. Her mother hadn't made it home.

"He's got bruises on his face," Lilly said, sobbing. "His hands are messed up too because he was trying to shield himself." She closed her eyes and shook her head. "He's locked himself in his room and won't come out. Probably because I went crazy when I came home and saw him."

"Where is your mother?" Forrest asked in a low voice.

"At her second job."

"She needs to come home."

"She's afraid she's going to lose her main job and—"

"She needs to come home *now*," Forrest said.

Lilly took a deep breath and lifted her cell phone. "What do I tell her?"

"Tell her you need her at home now," he said. "If you need me to talk to her, I will."

Lilly nodded. "I'll call her," she said and punched a button. "Mom," she said. "We need you to come home. We've had some problems." Silence followed. "I'd rather tell you when you get here. We're mostly okay, but we need you here."

When Lilly hung up, Forrest looked at her in approval. "Good job. Can you take me to your brother's room?"

"Sure, but he probably won't let you in," she said and guided him upstairs.

Forrest stood in the hall as Lilly knocked on the door. "Joey?"

"I'm not talking to you," he said through the door.

"Will you talk to Major Traub?" she asked.

A long silence followed. "No."

Forrest shrugged. "No problem. I'll talk to him. You can go back downstairs and wait for your mom with Angie."

Lilly nodded. "Okay, but I'm not sure that's going to help."

"We'll see," he said and waited until she descended the stairs. He knocked on the door. "Joey, it's me, Forrest Traub. You don't have to do the talking. I will," he said and leaned against the doorjamb.

"When I first entered the military, there was a guy who bullied several of us. He beat us up when no one was looking," he said. "We didn't want to rat on him. We were supposed to be a team," he said. "The army sent in a Special Forces guy to talk to us. We found out he had been bullied, too. Bullies need to be re-educated and retrained. They'll just bully someone else until they learn to act differently."

Forrest was quiet for several moments. "Yeah, so even though I was an adult, I was bullied."

He waited again. "My leg's killing me. Do you mind letting me in so I can sit down?"

The door immediately opened and Forrest walked inside toward the chair in his room. "Thanks," he said as he sat.

Joey kept his head lowered, but Forrest saw the bruises already forming on his forehead. He swore under his breath. "Some people just need to be totally reprogrammed."

"Yeah," Joey said. "If I tell, I'll be a rat."

"Yeah, but if you don't, this guy will never learn. And he'll bully someone else," Forrest said. "I'm betting there's someone at your school who wants to help whoever did this to you and more importantly, help you."

Joey glanced up, his eyes bloodshot and swollen. The sight made Forrest want to punch the guy who had done this to the kid.

"You have good stuff inside you. You're bigger than this. Hang on to that," he said.

Forrest heard female voices outside the door.

Joey rolled his eyes. "Oh, no. Mom's home."

A couple moments later, the rest of the women stormed Joey's room. Forrest sat silently in the background while his mother asked questions and Lilly cried. He met Angie's gaze. She seemed tense at first then relaxed.

After the interrogation wound down, Joey hid himself in his sleeves.

Joey's mother began to pace. "This is all my fault," she murmured. "I shouldn't have been working so much. I shouldn't have—"

"This is going to be okay," Forrest said. "Joey is going to talk to the school counselor, who will be appalled and will immediately enact an anti-bully program. Joey's bully will be supervised left and right and taught empathy. The entire school will improve as a result of Joey taking the proper action tomorrow. Right, Joey?"

Joey peeked above his arms. "Would you go with me?"

"Sure," Forrest said and shot Angie a vengeful grin. "It will be my pleasure."

A half hour later, Forrest escorted Angie to her pickup. "Interesting evening," he said, his leg aching like nobody's business.

"True," she said, stopping and looking up at him. "Thank you for coming. I think you really made a difference. I also think Joey will feel better talking about this to someone at school with you by his side."

She shrugged. "Well, anyone would feel better doing something tough with you by their side."

His heart jumped at her words. Her admiration, no it was far above admiration, meant more to him than he could have expected. "That was nice," he said.

"Just true, like you," she said. "If I were the type to throw myself at a man, I would do it now." She shot him a Delilah kind of smile. "But you and I both know I'm not that kind of woman."

"Right," he said and walked beside her to her truck, half wishing she *would* throw herself at him.

She turned toward him and smiled. "I knew you were pretty darn awesome the first time I met you, Forrest Traub. You just keep proving that over and over. G'night," she said. "I'll see you soon."

Forrest watched her get behind the wheel and drive away, and damn if he didn't wish he was going to the same place she was headed.

The next day, Forrest stood by Joey's side as he spoke to the counselor. Just as Forrest had predicted, the counselor was appalled. An anti-bully program would immediately be implemented. It wasn't his most mature thought, but he would have liked to beat the hell out of Joey's bully. He arranged with Joey to get together in a couple days. Forrest figured Joey's mom and sister would be hovering and Joey would be screaming for a break by then.

Leaving the school, he thought about calling

Angie, but he resisted the urge to call her and went to the local gym to work out. After the gym, he would go to his contract position at the architectural firm. By the time he finished his workout, though, he was exhausted. He grabbed a sandwich at a sub shop and walked toward the firm.

Halfway there, a loud shot rang out from the street. Forrest immediately went on the alert, reaching for his firearm. Which wasn't there. For a millimeter of a second, the street in front of him turned sideways. His heart pounded. He couldn't breathe.

He forced himself to take in air and his vision cleared. His mind cleared. The sound he'd heard had been that of a car backfiring. Not a warning shot from a gun. Everything was okay. Everyone was okay.

He took another deep breath and felt the unwelcome perspiration that always followed an episode. Damn this so-called syndrome. He wasn't in Iraq any longer. When would his mind and body know it?

Swiping the back of his hand across his damp forehead and above his upper lip, he began to talk to himself, assuring his body that it no longer needed to be on alert. He walked slowly to the office and inside the door.

"Hello, Forrest," the receptionist said. "It's good to see you. How are you doing?"

"Fine," he said. He just had to convince his brain of that fact.

It took awhile, but since there was an empty conference room available, Forrest took the room and calmed down enough to complete his work scheduled for the day. He left a little later than he'd intended, and his cell phone rang as he walked out the door.

"Forrest Traub," he said, after he saw Angie's number on his caller ID.

"Are you still downtown? I've been in class all day. How'd it go with Joey? I've been dying to know," Angie said.

"Not bad. He did a great job. You would have been proud of him. I was," he said.

"How did the counselor respond?" she asked.

"Very well," he said. "Honestly appalled. Good woman," he said. "I'll stay on top of it."

"So will I," Angie said. "Let me take you out for some hot chocolate tonight. We were interrupted last night."

"Not tonight," he began. "I—" He broke off when he heard her laughter and it wasn't via the phone. Glancing over his shoulder, he caught her just before she rushed him.

"But you have to," she insisted, smiling up at him.

Still dealing with his episode earlier this afternoon, he gently, but firmly pushed her away. He shook his head. "I'm not up for it tonight."

Her smile fell. "Aw, come on. It's not that big of a commitment."

"It's not about commitment," Forrest said. "I just want to be alone tonight."

Her eyebrows lifted in surprise. "Oh."

That *oh* held a wealth of hurt, but Forrest couldn't help Angie with it. He couldn't give her any hope. If anything, what had happened earlier today underscored that fact. Not that he had forgotten it, he reassured himself. "I'll walk you to your truck," he offered.

She immediately shook her head. "No need. I'll just head over to ROOTS to check on things."

"You shouldn't be walking around town in the dark," he said, and walked alongside her.

Angie gave a short laugh. "I walk around downtown by myself all the time. I'm strong and careful," she said, giving a toss of her hair.

"But you're also young and female," he said.

"Don't worry about me. I'll be okay," she said and ran into the dark.

With his bum leg, he couldn't go after her. And it irritated the hell out of him. One more reminder why he shouldn't encourage her. His injuries made him eons older. Angie needed a man who laughed easily and could run beside her. He would never be that man.

The sound of Angie's boots thumping against the payment echoed in her ears as she ran toward ROOTS. The sound and feeling of Forrest's rejection ripped through her. Foolish tears burned her eyes. He'd seemed so open to her lately. She'd fallen even more for him when he'd stepped forward to help Joey.

He'd seemed to enjoy their hot chocolate breaks. There had even been a few times when she'd felt him resisting the urge to touch her. She'd felt him wanting her. She'd seen it in his eyes. The electricity had hummed deliciously between them.

Or not? she wondered.

She'd been determined not to push him after the kiss they'd shared. The kiss he'd said they *shouldn't* have shared. For the first time since she'd met Forrest, a tiny sliver of doubt eked past her confidence that he would come around. He'd seemed so cold and distant tonight.

Her belief in her own feelings for Forrest, however, was rock solid.

Angie slowed to a walk and sighed. She was just going to have to be patient.

Two days later, she finalized the menu for the soldiers' families' dinner with Shane Roarke, the new super chef at Thunder Canyon Resort. This was going to be a crazy busy day because the community was holding Old Thunder Canyon Days downtown. Despite the threat of snow, crowds always came out to sample goodies from local shops and charities. A rancher sponsored an elephant for rides. For the truly brave, there would be ballroom dancing in the streets with accompaniment by the Thunder Canyon Community Orchestra. The ROOTS kids were taking orders for pumpkin bread loaves and pies for Thanksgiving.

It was midmorning and already the streets were cordoned off from traffic, so she parked several blocks from the city center and jogged to the ROOTS booth where several kids were giving away samples. "Hi there. How's it going?" she asked Brooke and Andrew, two of the ROOTS volunteers.

"We've got them once they taste it," Brooke said.

"Of course we do," Angie said.

"The only problem is the bakery shop has a booth three doors down from ours," Andrew said.

Angie made a face. "Well, darn. Do you want me to go out and direct people to our booth?"

"It can't hurt," Andrew said.

"Done," she said and took a poster out among the crowd. "Free pumpkin pie. Booth 117. Free pumpkin pie. Free pumpkin bread. Free pumpkin chocolate chip bread."

Angie kept shouting her invite for the next hour. Her voice began to sound raspy to her own ears, but she kept on. "Free pumpkin pie. Booth 117—"

"Sounds good to me," a familiar male voice said from behind her.

Angie whipped around to face Forrest. Her heart tripped over itself. "Hi," she said.

"Hi to you. Are you always in the middle of everything?" he asked.

She smiled. "I try. I like it better than looking from the outside in. What are you doing here?"

"I'm headed to work in about an hour," he said.

"Then you can get a free sample of pumpkin pie and order one from ROOTS," she said. "Booth—"

"One-seventeen," he said. "I heard you. What am I going to do with a pumpkin pie?"

"Eat it?" she asked. "We're taking orders. You can pick it up the day before Thanksgiving. Is someone fixing a Thanksgiving dinner for you? This would be the perfect gift to take as a guest."

"Are you sure you shouldn't be training to go into sales? You're so good you could sell ice cubes in a blizzard."

"You exaggerate, Major," she said.

"Not me," he said and music began to play. "Is that an orchestra?" he asked, clearly surprised.

Angie nodded. "And soon, there'll be dancing. In the street," she added. "Dare you to dance," she said impulsively, almost surprising herself with the challenge.

He shook his head. "It would be ugly," he said. "Very ugly."

"Double dare you," she said.

He shot her an uneasy look and shrugged. "I think I'll go order a pumpkin pie instead."

Angie sighed, wishing Forrest would make just a tiny move toward her. Just a tiny move was all it would take.

"What are you staring at, Angie?" Brad Graham, one of her old boyfriends, asked. "Come dance with me."

She shook her head. "No. I've gotta hawk for ROOTS. Find somebody else."

"You can take a break for a minute," he said. "Consider it your duty to the community."

"That's why I'm hawking for ROOTS," she said.

"Your voice is hoarse. Come on," he said, taking away her sign to lay it down and dragging her to the center of the street where several dancers already stood.

The orchestra switched into a number perfect for a tango. Angie swore under her breath and really hoped Forrest wasn't watching her dance in the arms of another man.

Chapter Five

Forrest went ahead and bought two pies and two loaves of pumpkin chocolate chip bread. He could give them to someone or maybe Antonia could freeze them. The ROOTS reps said the stuff could be frozen. He didn't know why he'd bought so much except that the idea of dancing with Angie did something strange to his gut.

"Hey, look. Angie's gonna rock it again this year," Andrew, a ROOTS volunteer, said.

What? Forrest swallowed the question and searched the crowd to the open street area. Angie was held in the arms of a young man. His stomach fell to his feet.

The music was romantic, filled with longing. It struck at the secret heart of him.

Her partner led her, pulling toward him, pushing her away, then pulling her back. Her hair whipped with her movements.

"She's really good, isn't she?" Andrew said beside him.

Forrest glanced at the guy who was watching with his arms crossed over his chest. "Yeah, she is. When did she learn this?"

"It was her brother and sister's idea. They made her learn all kinds of dances so she would be well-rounded. Her mother died when she was young," Andrew said.

"Thirteen," Forrest said, staring at Angie as she continued to dance. He couldn't quite force his gaze from her.

Andrew chuckled. "Poor Brad's always trying to get back with her."

"Back with her?" Forrest echoed, feeling his gut clench for what had to be the fifth time.

"Yeah, they were together for a while. Then he stepped out on her. She wrote off love. Brad works on her every chance he gets," Andrew said.

Brad bent Angie into a low dip and lowered his mouth toward hers. Forrest held his breath. Angie slid her hand around Brad's neck at the same time she turned her cheek to his mouth.

Andrew chuckled again. "Looks like it's still a no-go for Angie. Better luck next time, Brad."

Or not, Forrest thought, still watching Angie. When the crowd applauded, she gave a quick little curtsey and wave then darted into the crowd. Within seconds, she appeared in front of him. Her eyes rounded. "Oh, wow, you're still here."

"I bought pies," he said. "You're a helluva dancer."

"My brother and sister's fault. They wanted me to be socially acceptable. I don't think it worked," she said and gave a quick, breathless laugh.

"Your partner wasn't bad, either," he said.

"Depends on your point of view. I tried to get you to dance," she reminded him.

"Not my thing. Especially now," he said.

"You could shuffle," she said. "Shuffling is fun with the right person."

"What you were doing wasn't shuffling."

"Tango in a peacoat." She shrugged. "It was just classes. I wouldn't know what to do with an American AK-27."

He smiled. "AK-47," he corrected. "And that's Russian. Not American."

Angie blinked. "Right. That's what I meant," she said. "Want another taste of pumpkin pie?"

"I think I've already had enough," he said, but it was the image of Angie doing that sexy dance with Brad that was making his stomach turn. The expression on her face told him that she still saw him as a life-size G.I. Joe. "I'll never be much of a dancer, Angie. You're young. You should get a guy who can keep up with you on the dance floor," he said and walked away.

Seconds later, he felt a sharp tug on his arm. He turned swiftly, finding Angie staring him in the face.

"You just insulted me. To think that I would choose to be with a man because he's a good dancer?" Her face flushed with anger. "I'm not sixteen, so quit treating me that way. Have a nice day, and try not to act like a jerk to anyone else," she said and this time, she turned away from him.

Forrest stared after her, shocked at her response. She was always so sweet and understanding. She'd put up with his grumpiness like no one else had. He felt a different kind of discomfort knot in his gut. She'd just given him a verbal smack upside the head. Maybe he'd deserved it, but he needed to keep his distance from her. She really didn't deserve him insulting her, though. Over the past weeks, he'd learned she was a hard worker, harder than most people realized, and she had a heart of gold. He supposed everyone had their limit. Even sweet Angie.

He walked through the crowded streets to his office building. The receptionist was absent and he was relieved he wouldn't be forced to make conversation when he didn't feel like it. Sitting at his desk, he turned on his computer and tried to focus on his work. In the background of his mind, though, he kept picturing Angie's wounded, angry face. Guilt stabbed at him. She didn't deserve to endure his crankiness. She was a sweet woman. She deserved better treatment. Even from him.

After Angie was relieved by a volunteer willing to continue hawking, she went to the library and worked on a term paper. Despite the fact that she was still in a bad mood from her confrontation with Forrest, she decided to make a quick trip to ROOTS. Walking into the building, she saw several teens sitting in chairs and sipping hot chocolate. Happy to see Lilly and her brother, Joey, at one of the tables with some other students, she waved at them.

"Hi, Angie," the group said in near-unison.

The sound of their voices gave her a little lift. "Hi, guys," she said in return. "Everything going okay?"

"Except exams," one of the guys said. "It's like an oncoming train."

"Me, too," Angie said. "I'm in the middle of term papers. Do you know how many pumpkin pie orders we got today?"

"A ton," Lilly said. "We're going to have to turn into baking beasts."

"Block out the three days before Thanksgiving," Angie said.

"Will do," Lilly said.

Angie glanced at Joey. The bruises on his face were fading, thank goodness. "Good to see you," she said.

He nodded, but didn't smile. She understood. He had to look cool. Angie chatted with the volunteer on duty and learned exactly how many pumpkin pies ROOTS would be baking next week. It wasn't a ton, but it was a lot. She meandered around the room a little, but her restlessness took over, so she decided to go home.

Angie took the unusually long walk to her truck. She suspected it was over a mile and a half. It was after ten o'clock and snow had begun to fall. Shoving her hands into her pockets, she tried not to think about Forrest. It had been a great day. Aside from him. She'd made progress on her class assignments, ROOTS would make a nice chunk of change from the pumpkin pie sale and Joey had shown up at the center. Life was good, she told herself and stuck out her tongue to catch a snowflake.

She unlocked her truck and stepped inside, closing the door and locking it. Sticking her key in the ignition, she turned it and there was a strange gurgling noise. She frowned and turned her key again. The gurgling noise only lasted a second. Silence followed.

Crap, she thought and sighed. She thought about

going outside to ask someone for help and heard several voices including her brother and sister, tell her *no*. "Okay, okay," she muttered and dialed her brother's number. It went straight to voice mail.

Next she tried her sister. That went straight to voice mail, too. Angie scowled. It was late enough that her sister and brother could be sharing a romantic evening with their spouses. She hated to interrupt that, she thought wryly.

Angie tried a couple more people with no luck and wondered how she could be the only one by herself tonight. Her mind turned to Forrest. She suspected he was by himself tonight. She suspected he was awake, or if not, his cell phone was on. He might even answer it. After the way he'd talked to her today, she'd rather walk home than call Forrest.

She sat in the car a couple more minutes, drumming her fingers on the steering wheel. It wasn't getting any warmer. She dialed her brother again, and her sister. No luck for her. Maybe they were getting lucky, she thought. She turned the key in the ignition and got nothing still.

She exhaled and her breath created a visible vapor. Reluctantly surrendering, she punched in Forrest's cell. She heard two rings and almost hung up.

"Hey. Forrest Traub. Is that you, Angie?"

"Yes," she said in a low voice. "My car is dead."

"Okay," he said. "Where are you? I'll be right there."

"Corner of Main and Turner," she said. "I wouldn't have bothered you, but—"

"I know you wouldn't have called me if you could have found anyone else," he said with a rough chuckle. "Hang on. I'll be there as soon as I can."

Angie stared at her phone then tossed it on the seat beside her. She drummed her fingertips on the steering wheel again, tempted to make a run for it. If she ran full force, she could be home in twenty-five minutes. Maybe.

This really sucked. She preferred to have Forrest crawl toward her in complete humility. He would lower himself on bended knee, which was currently an impossible position for him with his injured leg. Then he would beg her forgiveness for being such a terrific jerk.

Then he would profess his love for her. He would tell her how much he needed her and...

Okay, that was total fantasy. But it had been fun.

Headlights flashed from behind her and she bit her lip. She hoped she just needed a jump for her battery. Angie waited until Forrest pulled his truck beside hers and walked to her driver's side window. She opened her door. "Hi," she said. "Thanks for coming."

"Least I could do after treating you so badly today.

Let's try your battery first," he said and moved to the front of the trucks.

Stunned at his almost-apology, she stared after him. So this was payback, she suspected. His way of making up for being a meanie earlier today. She stepped outside her truck and joined him in the cold night where snow fell.

"How many people did you call before me?" he asked.

"I lost count after the first five," she said, crossing her arms over her chest to keep herself warm.

He scrubbed at his chin. "Go ahead and try to start it."

Angie returned to the cab of the truck and turned the key and mashed the accelerator. Over the next several moments, she tried again and again. She took a break then tried again. No luck.

Forrest walked to her window. "Sorry. It's not the battery."

"I got that impression," she said. "What do you think it is?"

"Maybe the alternator," he said. "I'm not sure. You'll need to get it into a garage. It's late tonight. You can get a tow first thing in the morning. I could tow you if you want."

She nodded. "This is very inconvenient. I have a packed schedule tomorrow."

"I can help," he offered. "I just have the meeting for veterans at the hospital."

"Nice of you to offer," she said.

"The least I can do," he said. "Listen, I shouldn't have been so—" He paused. "I shouldn't have been—"

"Such a jerk?" she suggested.

He lifted an eyebrow. "Would it feel better to slap me?"

She recoiled at the thought. "I wouldn't do that."

He extended his hand. "Let me take you home. I'll cart you tomorrow as much as I can."

She accepted his assistance and got into his truck. He revved the engine and turned up the heat, as he headed toward her home. After a few moments, she felt the rush of warmth. "That feels good," she said. Then, after a moment, "When did you realize you'd been a jerk?"

"Three steps after I walked away from you," he said. "You deserve better treatment. You're a great person. You do good things. You're good to everyone."

"Yep, that's me. Tinker Bell."

He shot her a quick glance. "I was trying to be sincere."

"Don't try too hard," she said. "I still say you could shuffle."

Forrest clenched his jaw. "Like I said, you deserve better."

"And I decide what better is. Right?" she said. "Better is relative. I bet my tango is nowhere near as good as your ability to operate an AK-27."

Forrest chuckled. "AK-47," he said. "And like I told you before, that's a Russian weapon."

"Exactly," she said. "That's what I meant to say."

"Yeah," he said. "No offense, Tinker Bell, but I don't want you in charge of issuing weapons."

"No problem," she said. "I've just got a few shotguns and pistols in the hall closet. I haven't touched them."

Forrest swore under his breath. "We'll take care of that soon," he said.

"Why? Some of them don't even work," she said.

"That's why," Forrest said. "You need to know what your weapons can and cannot do. What you don't know about the weapons you own is dangerous."

"You sound like an army major or something," she said.

"You live by yourself," he said. "This isn't a joking matter."

"I keep a baseball bat under my bed. That should count for something, shouldn't it?"

Forrest clenched his jaw again. Silence followed.

"Are you counting? What number have you reached?"

He almost grinned as he pulled into her driveway

and stopped the truck. He turned to her. "Half of you is an angel and half of you is a tormentor. I can't help wanting to protect you, but at the same time, I don't want to get in your way. You're doing a lot of good."

"Well, that's nice of you. But, Forrest, you need to remember I've survived twenty-three years without you. As much as I appreciate you helping me with my truck, I could have run home in the snow. It wouldn't have been fun, but I could have done it," she said.

"So why didn't you?" he asked.

"Because I knew you'd answer your phone," she finally admitted. "I knew you'd come. And I knew my brother and sister would be really pissed at me if I wasn't safe. Although I can run pretty fast when my adrenaline is turned up high."

"I'm sure you can, but I'm really glad you called me. And I hope you'll call me again if something like this happens again."

"I hope it won't," she muttered and opened her door. Her heart was thumping in her throat. The expression on his face was hard for her to take. He wanted her, but hated the fact. "Thank you again for answering and for coming to help me."

He surprised her by joining her. She'd thought he would just watch her from the truck. "I'll call you in the morning. We can figure out what to do with your truck."

"Yeah, I just hope it's not too expensive, or I'll have to hold my own bake sale," she said, chuckling at the thought. The snow fell in soft flakes. "Isn't it beautiful?" she said. "It's so pretty when it falls like this instead of sideways."

"You mean, instead of a blizzard?" he asked.

She nodded and stuck out her tongue to catch a snowflake.

"You still do that?" he asked. "I haven't tried to catch a snowflake on my tongue since I was a kid."

"Well, you should," she said sternly. "If I live to be eighty, I'll still be catching snowflakes on my tongue."

"Why?" he asked, and she felt his gaze on her from head to toe. His gaze wasn't sexual. Darn it. It was more of curiosity. Almost wonder.

"Because it's fun and it's free, and it's important to try to have fun every day of your life. Did you know that some experts say that play is the secret to happiness?"

"I don't have time to play all day," he said. "I have more important things to do."

She turned to meet his gaze. "Maybe that's why you get cranky. I dare you to catch a snowflake on your tongue. Betcha can't do it," she said.

He rested his hands on his hips and gave a half roll of his eyes. "Of course I can do it."

"I don't know that. *You* don't even know that because it's been so long since the last time. It does require some technique. Double dare you," she said.

"This is crazy," he said.

"But you're thinking about it," she said, unable to smother a smile.

"Okay, okay," he said and stuck out his tongue.

"You need to stick out your tongue farther and lift up your head," she said.

"Crazy," he muttered again, but she could tell he was now determined to do it.

He made a few modifications and three seconds later, he caught a snowflake. He met her gaze. "Got one."

"It was fun, wasn't it?"

"Silly," he said, walking toward her door.

"But fun," she insisted.

"Yeah," he said.

"That enthusiasm looks good on you," she said then gave him a quick salute and walked inside her house. Angie leaned her back against the door and took several deep breaths. The fact that he had answered her call, the fact that he had come to help her grabbed at something deep inside her. She'd tried to make light of it, but the truth was his appearance tonight was one more thing that made him different. One more thing that convinced her that he was the one she wanted.

He wasn't immune to her. She knew it. He might hate the fact, but he cared about her far more than he wanted.

After a restless night, Forrest dragged himself out of bed and drove to Angie's house. He sucked down his second cup of coffee as he pulled into her driveway and turned off the engine to his truck and opened the driver's side door. Before he could put one foot out, Angie darted from the house.

"I'm coming. I'm coming," she said, carrying two steaming cups and a backpack flung over her shoulder.

"G'mornin'," she said with a big smile and handed him a cup of coffee before she went to the passenger side of the truck.

Forrest held a cup in each hand and stared at one then the other.

Angie bounded into the seat beside him. "Oops. Do you need me to take that?" she asked.

He shook his head and swallowed the three drops left in the one he'd brought then tossed the cup into the back floorboard. "No. Thanks. I needed a third cup."

Her eyes widened. "Whoa. How long have you been awake?"

"I'm awake, but not nearly as perky as you are."

"I didn't dry my hair all the way, so ice crystals

are forming on my scalp. You'd be surprised how quick that'll make you wake up."

He grinned and took a drink of coffee. "This has some of that sweet stuff in it," he said.

"Hazelnut. You don't have to drink it if you don't like it," she said.

"After three cups of coffee, what's a cup of sugar?" he said and pulled out of her driveway.

"Where are we going?" he asked.

"College library," she said.

"What are we doing about your truck?"

"I called a tow service. They're hauling it to the garage," she said.

"I told you I could do that for you," he said.

"You have enough to do today. Besides, they won't charge me for the tow because their kids were once involved with ROOTS," she said.

"Nice connections," he said.

"They didn't help me last night," she said then shot him a lopsided smile. "Both my brother and sister called me this morning. At 6:00 a.m. They were panicked. I told them they were a little late. They both said they went to bed early. Yeah, I knew what they were doing while I was suffering in a dead car in the snow."

He chuckled at her mock-dark tone. "Do I hear a touch of resentment from Miss Perfect?"

"I'm not Miss Perfect. And no resentment from

me. Both my brother and sister sacrificed too much for me. I'm glad they're happy. Really," she said.

"But?" he prompted, hearing something else in her voice.

"But nothing," she said.

Forrest let the silence sit between them. It was an awkward, uncomfortable silence.

"Okay, the truth is, I miss them sometimes. They've found the loves of their lives, and sometimes I feel stuck in Neutral," she said.

"Just because you're not racing forward doesn't mean you're stuck in Neutral," he said as he pulled into the parking lot of the college library. "Look at how much you're helping the kids at ROOTS. You're making a difference in people's lives. Hell, you've made a difference in my life," he admitted.

Her face brightened.

"But don't read anything into that," he warned her.

She bit her lip, but her eyes didn't dim one bit. "Of course not," she said. "Thanks for picking me up this morning."

"No problem. When do you need your next transfer?" he asked.

"I'm good," she said. "I'm hoping the garage will be able to fix my truck this morning."

He felt an irrational flash of disappointment. "It's not a big deal."

"You coming to get me last night and picking

me up this morning was a big deal. Your hero work is done, at least for now," she said with a smile and leaned toward him. She pursed her lips and pulled back as if she remembered to stop behind the hard line he'd drawn.

"Hope the caffeine doesn't put you on the ceiling during your meeting with the veterans," she said.

He shook his head and grinned. "Nah, I've got time to crash and burn before then."

"You didn't sleep well last night?" she asked, concern deepening her brown eyes.

He shrugged. "It's not that unusual."

"Is it because I dragged you out so late to help me?"

"Nah," he said. "I overdid my workout at the gym and was paying for it."

She frowned. "Don't you have pain meds for that?"

He shook his head. "I don't use them. I don't want to depend on them. Most of the time a hot shower does the job. I'll slack off the next couple days."

She smiled. "You don't know the meaning of slacking off, but if you hang around with me a little more, maybe you can learn how to be more of a slacker." She opened the door and stepped outside.

"Faker. You're no slacker," he said.

"Have a nice day, Major," she said and skipped through the snow to the library door.

He rubbed his jaw then took a sip of the hazelnut coffee, staring at Angie until she disappeared from his view. He was starting to wonder if she was part fairy, and even he knew that was nuts.

Chapter Six

Two days later when Forrest hadn't shown up at ROOTS or called her, Angie gave in and called him.

"Forrest Traub," he said in a croaky voice.

"Oh, no, you're sick," she said. "That's what I was afraid of. A bunch of the ROOTS kids have come down with something nasty. I'll bring you some soup," she said.

"Not necessary. I'm getting better," he said.

"You sound horrible," she said.

"Thank you."

"I'm bringing soup," she told him.

"Angie, don't. I don't want you to get this," he said. "It sucks."

"I know, but I've already been exposed ten times over. I don't get sick these days, thank goodness. When I was young, I came down with everything. I swear if it was anywhere in the state of Montana, it seemed to find me. I guess I built up immunity from that. So, I'll be over in two hours. Go take a nap. Can I get you anything else?" she asked.

"Nah, I'm fine," he said and coughed.

"Liar," she said. "How about some throat lozenges and that stuff that numbs the back of your throat?"

"Well, if you really don't mind," he said.

"Not at all. Favorite juice?"

"Orange," he said.

"Crackers?"

"Yes," he said.

"Does your brother know you're sick?" she asked, unsettled that it appeared that no one had checked in on him.

"He and Antonia went to visit my parents. They'll be back the day after tomorrow," he said. "I'm helping with the horses and the ranch until then."

Horrified, she couldn't hold back a sound of frustration. "You've been *working* the ranch while you've been sick?"

"It's not that big of a deal," he croaked.

"What is it with you? Are you one of those people who isn't happy unless you're chewing glass?" she asked.

He gave a hoarse laugh. "Funny you should say that. That's exactly how my throat feels."

"Two hours," she said. "Take a nap."

Angie hustled to make a pot of regular chicken soup and chicken enchilada soup. She thought he might be ready for the latter when his condition improved. While baking a pan of brownies, she called a couple of the ROOTS teen guys and asked them to help out at the ranch while Forrest recovered.

With the teens and soup in tow, she drove up to Forrest's rooming house. She turned to Chad and Max. "I gotta warn you. He's not going to want your help, but he needs it."

Chad, a fourteen-year-old, who had become deeply impressed with Forrest when he'd talked with the group, looked worried. "Should he be in the hospital?"

"I hope not, but we'll find out," she said and got out of the truck. The boys helped her carry the soup and other necessities. She knocked on the front door.

A couple seconds later, Forrest opened the door and she winced at the sight of him. His eyes were bloodshot with circles beneath and he was pale. "Oh my, you need to lie down. You look terrible."

He gave a grim half grin. "Thanks. You look great, too."

"I didn't mean to offend," she said and rushed inside with the boys. "Are you sure we shouldn't take you to the doctor?"

GET 2 BOOKS

We'd like to send you two *Harlequin® Special Edition* novels absolutely free. Accepting them puts you under no obligation to purchase any more books.

HOW TO GET YOUR 2 FREE BOOKS AND 2 FREE GIFTS

1. Return the reply card today, and we'll send you two *Harlequin Special Edition* novels, absolutely free! We'll even pay the postage!

2. Accepting free books places you under no obligation to buy anything, ever. Whatever you decide, the free books and gifts are yours to keep, free!

3. We hope that after receiving your free books you'll want to remain a subscriber, but the choice is yours—to continue or cancel, any time at all!

EXTRA BONUS

**You'll also get two free mystery gifts!
(worth about $10)**

FREE!

▼ DETACH AND MAIL CARD TODAY! ▼

"I'm pretty sure it's viral," he said. "Came on fast and hard and that's what they do. Nice of all of you to bring the soup."

"And a few other things," she said, guiding everyone to the small kitchen. "The boys are here to help with the horses."

Forrest shook his head. "I'm not sending them out there to shovel stalls. I can take care of that tomorrow."

"You must be counting on a miraculous recovery," she said, not even trying to hide her doubt.

"I don't stay down long," he told her. "I never have."

"I'm sure you don't, but—"

"Chad and I don't mind shoveling stalls," Max said. "We both have experience with it, so it's not like it will take us long. Angie can give you some soup and maybe we can steal a couple brownies after we finish."

The two boys didn't give Forrest much of a chance to argue as they raced out of the house. He frowned at Angie. "That wasn't necessary," he said.

"Go sit down while I heat up some soup for you. What do you want to drink?" she asked as she warmed the soup in the microwave.

"I've got some water," he said, but didn't follow her instructions to leave the room. "You did too much. It's not like I'm on death's door," he said, his voice raw.

"Maybe not, but you sure sound like it," she said. "Do you want to eat in here at the table or in the den?"

"Den," he said and walked into the next room.

She handed him the bowl of soup along with a few crackers. He took a spoonful and closed his eyes. When he sat that way for several seconds, she wondered if something was wrong. "Are you okay?"

He opened his eyes and met her gaze. "This is the best soup in the world."

She smiled, feeling a rush of pleasure. "Well, that's good to hear. It's my mom's recipe." She sat beside him with her bag of goodies. "I've already put orange juice in the fridge. And some ginger ale, because ginger ale always tastes good when you're sick. I put honey on your table, because a friend of mine told me that a spoonful coats your throat. Here's something you spray to numb it and two different kinds of lozenges. Oh, and ibuprofin, which reduces swelling and fever," she said as she shook the box.

"Are you sure you didn't forget anything?"

She frowned. "I hope not, but—"

He waved his hand, interrupting her. "I was joking."

"Oh, okay. Well, go ahead and finish that soup. It seems to be making you feel better and that's what's important." She got up and went to the kitchen, rummaging in his refrigerator to make sure he was adequately stocked. She poured a glass of ginger ale for him with ice and returned to the den to find he had demolished the soup.

"More?" she asked.

"Maybe," he said, his voice sounding slightly less croaky. "I'll wait a few minutes first."

She set the ginger ale on a coaster on the coffee table. "You know you need to keep drinking. I would have fixed you tea, but you don't seem the type."

"I'm not," he said. "Don't get too close. I don't want you to get sick."

"Oh, I don't get sick," she said.

He shot her a doubtful glance. "You said that before. What?"

"I really don't. I got sick all the time as a child. I told you this on the phone. I don't get sick anymore," she said.

"Must be nice," he grumbled.

"Clean living and positive thinking," she said in a sly tone.

"A saint," he said.

"I never said that," she retorted. "My sister always told me to change my pillowcase every night when I was sick. I'll change yours," she said, rising.

"I can do that," he said.

"But I'm here," she said. "When you're really starting to improve, that's when you change your sheets."

"Sounds like a system," he said.

"You would have one too if you had a kid that got sick every time someone said boo," she said as she left the den. She wandered down the hall to his bedroom and tried not to feel as if she were intruding. Opening the closet, she found a neatly folded stack of linens. She took a couple pillowcases and changed them with the current ones then returned to the den.

"I don't need you to make such a fuss over me," he told her.

"I'm not. I'm just acting like someone who cares for you, although I'm tempted to put my hand on your tummy to see if you have a fever," she said.

He blinked. "What?"

"You can put your hand on someone's forehead to check for fever, but the tummy is a better measurement if you're not using a thermometer."

"You don't really think you're going to take my temperature," he said.

"Well, no," she said, and her gaze dipped to what she knew was his flat abdomen. "But I thought about it."

Despite the fact that he was clearly sick and feverish, she saw a flicker of desire in his eyes. Unless she was hallucinating, and she didn't think she was.

Forrest picked up the glass of ginger ale and took a sip. He winced as he swallowed.

"Honey," she said, rushing to the kitchen. "You need honey."

He lifted his hand. "I'm okay."

"Just try it," she said, digging a teaspoon from a drawer and grabbing the honey.

When she returned he was standing, looking at her with a skeptical glance.

"Just try it," she urged.

He shot her a long-suffering glance. "Okay."

She poured the honey into the spoon and lifted it to his mouth. He swallowed it down.

She waited.

He swallowed again. "Not bad."

She smiled. "Yay."

"But the soup is way better," he said.

The boys burst into the front door. "Horse poop's all gone. Any brownies left?" Chad asked.

"Are you sure you want brownies right now?"

"Oh, yeah," Max said. "We were talking about them the whole time."

Angie exchanged a glance with Forrest. He chuckled then coughed and winced.

"Alrighty. Wash your hands and come get your brownies," Angie said and turned toward the kitchen. She lifted foil from the pan and gave each teen two brownies. They wolfed them down. "Okay, one more each," she said and gave them another.

"Good. Mmm," Chad said.

"Yeah," Max said, rubbing his stomach. "Mmm."

"Glad you liked them," she said and noticed that Forrest had followed them into the kitchen. "What else can we do for you?"

"Nothing," Forrest said. "I've got the best soup in the world and a bunch of meds I don't need. Plus I don't have to muck the stalls tomorrow."

"We refilled the water and feed, too," Max said.

"Thanks," Forrest said.

"If you're sure," Angie said.

"I'm sure," he said, his voice breaking up.

"You need more honey."

"Soup," he corrected.

She felt the oddest longing in the world to stay and nurse him back to health. *As if he would let her.*

"I'll call you later," she said and waved her finger at him. "And you better answer."

"I will," he said. "Thanks for everything. You guys did too much." He paused. "But I'm not sharing one drop of that soup."

She wanted to embrace him, hold him tight, but she knew he wouldn't want that. Angie took a deep breath. "Are you sure you're okay?"

"I'm better than I was before you came. And tomorrow I don't have to do anything due to Chad and Max," Forrest said.

Chad and Max puffed up their chests. "It was nothing," Max said.

"But those brownies were awesome."

Angie laughed. "Okay, let's get out of here so Forrest can rest. Get well," she said.

He nodded. "I'll do that," he murmured and escorted them to the door.

Three hours later, after Angie had forced herself to wait out the time, she dialed Forrest's cell phone. Four rings later, he finally picked up.

"Forrest Traub," he muttered.

"This is Angie. How are you doing?"

"I don't know. I was asleep," he mumbled.

"Oh, I'm sorry," she said, wincing. "Go back to sleep."

"Okay," he said, but paused a moment. "I'm better," he said. "Thanks for coming."

"You're welcome. Good night," she said and disconnected the call. She still wanted to go over to his house and help him, but she knew he didn't want her there. Angie longed for the day when he would want her around day and night. She couldn't help feeling they'd taken another step closer, but they had a long way to go.

Forrest sank back against his pillow with the fresh pillowcase. Then he rose again and took a sip of water from the cup on his nightstand. He felt like someone was sticking a thousand needles in his throat.

Maybe he should try some of the stuff Angie had left for him.

Rising from the bed, he went to the kitchen where he'd left all the meds Angie had brought him. One of them was a spray that supposedly numbed the throat. He was game. He sprayed several times. Lord, that stuff tasted foul. He grabbed a couple lozenges and resolved not to swallow. Maybe that would save him a little pain.

As he slid back into bed, he remembered what she'd said about putting her hand to his forehead. Then he imagined her hand over his abdomen. His gut tightened at the thought. He tightened in other ways, too.

Angie was an odd mix of innocence, earnestness and sexy, he thought as he drifted off to sleep. *His fevered mind traveled to the image of her sliding her hands over his body. Soon enough, her clothes would disappear and she rubbed her naked body against his.*

Her breasts were taut, her skin silky soft, her lips moist and welcoming. He slid his thigh between hers and she was wet and welcoming there, too. She wriggled against him, making needy, sexy sounds. The sensation of her nude body against his took his breath away. His heart skipped once, twice, three times.

He slipped the fingers of one hand through her

hair and pressed his other hand against her bottom so that she was as close to him as she could get. He rubbed against her intimately, feeling himself grow harder and harder.

She clung to him, thrusting her wet femininity against him.

He couldn't resist one moment longer and pushed inside her. She was like a velvet glove around him.

"Give me you," she whispered. "Give me all of you."

Forrest thrust inside her, filling her. She felt so good.

Forrest awakened hot, hard and bothered. He swore in frustration. Angie again. He hadn't touched her since that kiss they'd shared, yet his body seemed determined to torment him. If dreaming about her got him this worked up, he wondered what having sex with her would do. He was finding it more and more difficult to keep his hands off of her.

Telling himself not to think about Angie and her effect on him, he settled back down and took several deep breaths. When he closed his eyes, he forced himself to think about blueprints. He fell back to sleep within seconds.

Hours later, Forrest's throat awakened him. He swallowed and winced, automatically reaching for the glass of water on his nightstand. Sitting up, he gulped it down. After several swallows, the pain in his throat slightly abated.

He took a breath then drank some more water and almost felt normal.

Almost.

Rising from the bed, Forrest took a hot shower and dressed in sweat pants and a T-shirt. Despite all his protests the day before, he was damn glad he didn't have to shovel the stalls today. Afterward, he collapsed on the sofa and turned on the television. He didn't care what was on. He just wanted something to numb his mind. Cartoons were the perfect choice.

Five minutes into the show, a knock sounded at the door. Forrest pulled his aching body from the couch to answer the door. After a quick glance through the peephole, he saw Angie and opened the door.

"What are you doing here?" he asked.

"I thought you might like some breakfast. Bacon, tomato and cheese omelet work for you?"

"I won't eat that much. I'm not hungry," he said.

"I'll fix it and you can decide," she said, scooting past him to the kitchen.

"I really don't want a big breakfast," he said.

"This won't be big," she countered and brought him a glass of orange juice and two ibuprofin.

"This is almost *smothering*," he said and downed the pills and orange juice.

"It's a caring friend," she corrected. "Now relax."

Moments later, she delivered a delicious omelet

with buttered toast on the side. He surprised himself with how much he consumed.

"How did that happen?" he asked. "I didn't think I could eat that much."

"I had a feeling you might wake up hungry this morning," she said with a self-satisfied expression.

"How did you know?" he demanded.

"You weren't eating the way you should when you first got sick. When you stopped feeling quite so bad, you got hungry again," she said.

"How would you know that when you never get sick?" he asked.

"Instinct," she said and picked up his nearly empty plate. "You'll be ready for a nap soon."

"How do you know that?" he asked.

"Do you really need to ask?" she asked.

"Instinct," he said, refusing to admit that he already felt drowsy. "That's bull."

"So right," she said. "You want to watch TV in your bedroom?"

He scowled. "I'm not going to sleep."

She nodded. "That's fine. Would you like something else to drink?"

He realized he was being cranky and ungrateful when he had every reason to be happy and thankful. "I think I'll watch TV in the bedroom."

He could see that she was determined to keep her face a blank palette. "That will work. It's best for you to be comfortable."

"I won't be there long," he told her as he walked to the bedroom. "I'll go down to check out the horses in just a little while."

She nodded. "Yes. Of course you will."

Forrest slid under his covers with his hand on the remote control. He watched the morning news and suddenly he fell asleep. Or into a coma.

Hours later, he awakened with the television on mute. His throat ached slightly. He wondered where the hell the time had gone.

Rising from his bed, he took a quick sip of water and walked toward the den where he heard the sound of a television. She glanced up at him. "Hey, how are you?"

"You gave me a sleeping pill," he accused her.

She shook her head. "No way. You just relaxed enough to doze. That was all."

He frowned.

"Before that, you were fighting the virus. Now, you're catching up with your rest."

He shot her a glance full of doubt. "Sounds like bull to me."

"You needed the sleep. Believe it or not, my being here helped you relax. I was your warrior woman."

He rolled his eyes. "If that isn't the biggest bunch of—"

"The important thing is that you rested. Would you like some soup now?"

Forrest's stomach growled.

"I'll take that as a yes," she said and rose from the sofa. "Have a seat. I'll bring you some apple cider while you wait."

A moment later, she brought him a mug of cider. He took a sip and relished the warmth on his throat. A bit later, she brought him a steaming bowl of chicken soup. He immediately abandoned the cider for the soup. He spooned the soup into his mouth and groaned in relief. The second spoonful bathed his throat again.

"This is so good," he muttered and downed more.

After several more spoonfuls, Forrest finished the soup and leaned his head back against the sofa. A few seconds passed, and he looked up at Angie.

"How the hell did I get so tired?"

"Your body is fighting an infection," she said. "We just need to help it. How do you feel now?"

"Like I need a nap," he said. "But if I go to sleep now, I won't be able to sleep later."

She nodded. "Okay. Let's go for a walk, then."

He paused then nodded. "I'm game."

They bundled up and trudged through the snow to the stables. Forrest gave the horses fresh water. "They need to be ridden or they'll get green, but I'm not the guy for that right now," he said as he rubbed the muzzle of one of the horses. "Antonia does a great job with these guys, but she just had a baby and the weather has made things even more tough. I may have to give my brother a nudge to ride these babies more often."

"Do you miss riding them?" she asked.

"I miss everything I used to be able to do without thinking twice," he said, rubbing the horse again. "At the same time, I'm damn grateful I can walk. I'm grateful I'm living."

Angie met his gaze. "I am, too," she said.

His gut clenched at her expression and he glanced at her then looked back at the horse. "Sometimes it's hard not to think about the guys who didn't make it," he said as faces of those who had died traveled through his mind.

"I can't begin to imagine," Angie said.

Forrest nodded. "Yeah, I get frustrated. I can get cranky. But I know I'm damn lucky. I'm alive."

Angie slid her arm over his. "I'm glad you're alive. I think you underestimate your effect on others."

"There's a weird pressure I feel to fix things," he said. "If it's wrong, I need to make it right."

"Like you did with Joey," she said. "And I've pushed you into helping me."

He thought about how withdrawn he'd been before Angie had burst into his life. "Could have been worse."

She nodded. "I think we could say that the rest of our lives."

He nodded. "Yeah," he said, remembering that she had lost both of her parents by the time she was a teenager.

"Time to go back," she said. "More soup and you'll be headed for la-la land."

"I need to stay awake a little longer," he said.

"I'll do what I can," she said. "Maybe some tap dancing or a rerun of *Project Runway*."

"The latter would be torture," he said.

"But if I asked your opinion or promised a quiz at the end of the show, you would be forced to stay awake," she said as they walked outside the barn toward the boardinghouse.

"If you were a cruel woman," he said.

"Cruel?" she said. "But you want me to keep you awake."

"It's a quandary," he said.

"Well, I suppose I could slap you," she said. "Would you like that?"

"Not really," he said. "But *Project Runway* could feel like sixty slaps."

"Sucks to be you," she said and brushed a kiss against his cheek.

He met her gaze. "Not really," he said and they walked in the front door.

The blast of warmth hit Angie as they entered the den. "Even I would fall asleep in this nice cozy temperature."

"What do you mean?"

"I mean, we're going to have to play charades or something to stay awake," she said. "Or maybe we could go for another walk."

"After more of your soup," he said.

Forrest almost nodded off in his soup.

"One more walk," she said, giving him a nudge as his eyes closed.

"You're a hard woman," he said as she handed him his jacket.

"You'll thank me in the morning," she told him. "You may often have a hard time falling asleep, but you won't tonight."

He pushed his hands through the sleeves of his jacket and they walked outside. She watched him suck in a quick, harsh breath.

"Damn cold," he said.

"But beautiful," she said, looking up at the sky. It looked like an endless indigo carpet of diamonds. "This is one of the great things about Montana. Big sky, night or day."

He looked up and nodded. "You're right."

He took another breath, but this one seemed deeper and easier.

"How do you like that crunchy snow?" she asked.

"I need to get used to it," he said as they walked toward the driveway. "We won't get a thaw for a long time."

"Oh, we could get an early thaw, but it would be a fake-out," she said. "The second we relax…"

"It would snow again," he said and stopped to look up at the moon again. "I remember seeing that same moon while I was in Iraq. I didn't feel the same about it then. The moon kept us from hiding. The moon revealed our position to the enemy."

"But now, it's beautiful," she said. "Now you don't need to hide or worry about concealing your position from the enemy."

She felt him take an easy inhalation. "Being with you makes me look at the world in a different way. Being with you makes me remember the good things about the sun and the moon and the stars."

His words grabbed at her heart. "I'm glad," she said. "And I'm hoping I can bore you enough to sleep the whole night through."

Chapter Seven

Forrest awakened the next morning after dawn. By the slant of the sun through the window curtain, he suspected it was way after dawn. He inhaled deeply and was pleased that it wasn't still dark. Angie had worn him out. Thank goodness.

He assessed his body from head to toe and noticed he didn't hurt all over. Just his leg ached. His usual *good-morning wake-up call* since the IED had changed his life and taken others.

Slowly rising, he was relieved that he didn't have a fever. He knew without Angie touching his forehead or belly. Although, he damn well would have welcomed her touch, despite the fact that he shouldn't.

Forrest went to the shower, the hot water soothed him at the same time it refreshed him. He forced himself to turn it off and exit the shower. Cool air rushed over his naked body. He shaved his two-day-old beard and rinsed his face with cold water. Rubbing deodorant under his arms, he pulled on a T-shirt and underwear and left the bathroom.

The air in the house was still cool which made it easy for him to pull on his jeans and a cotton sweater. He remembered the days when he'd awakened to dress in his uniform. Now, he had a different purpose. Forrest wasn't always sure what that purpose was, but he was working on it. Every day, he was working on it. Every day, he was sucked into new ways of making a difference. Back in Iraq, he'd never dreamed of what civilians back home needed other than his military service. Now, he was up-front with all the messy problems of life in the States.

In some ways, civilians had it harder than the military. The army dealt with the immediate threat of wartime. Civilians faced everyday threats: illness, financial difficulty, crappy weather, undependable cars. Daily life took more persistence. War could take a life in a moment. A tour of duty in Iraq lasted twelve to fifteen months at the most. A tour of duty in civilian life could last forever.

He did a light workout then decided he needed to go into town. He'd been cooped up too long in the rooming house. Cabin fever. His brother and Antonia would arrive home later in the day. He drove his truck into town and grabbed a cappuccino. The sugar gave him an extra boost of energy. The barista was extra friendly, but he was focused on the caffeine and sugar.

He sat down at a table and looked out the window. The sun shone brightly, but the temperature was so cold the snow wouldn't be melting any time soon. Forrest was glad he'd brought his sunglasses. From his peripheral vision, he saw the barista put a piece of paper on his table. He didn't pick it up, but saw her name and phone number. Danielle, he saw.

Somehow, he wasn't the least bit tempted. Instead of Danielle, he saw Angie with her big brown eyes. Angie, with the big hugs and bigger heart.

Forrest swore under his breath. Lord help him, he couldn't look at another woman without thinking of Angie. What was he supposed to do now?

He remembered walking in the moonlight with her last night. His leg had ached like a mother, but she had chatted on and on, until finally, they'd walked back to the rooming house.

Moments after they'd arrived, she'd encouraged him to change into his bedclothes. Soon after, she'd told him to go to bed. Seconds later, he'd fallen asleep.

The young barista flitted beside his table again. "Call me," she said in a low voice.

"Can't," he said, unwilling to lead her on. "I'm out on parole. I have to go back to the big house this afternoon."

The blonde blinked at him. "The big house?"

"Yeah, but maybe after I get out for good," he said.

She bit her lip. "That's okay. Have a nice day."

Forrest chuckled under his breath as he left. He took his cappuccino and returned to his truck. He decided to see if Angie was at the college library and drove into the parking lot. Sure enough, her truck was there. So, despite the fact that she'd been taking care of him, she'd still needed to take care of her studies.

Forrest walked to a different coffee shop one block over and bought a cappuccino for Angie then returned to the college library. Strolling inside, he searched for Angie, but had to walk all the way to the back to find her.

"Hiya," she said when she saw him.

"What are you doing here?" he asked and set the coffee cup next to her.

"Wrapping up a few things," she said and took the lid off the cup and sniffed it. Her face was the picture of ecstasy. "Heaven," she said. "This is heaven."

"Or, you're just desperate," he said with a chuckle. "How long have you been here?"

"Two hours. I took a nap after I got home from seeing you."

"Why didn't you tell me you should be studying?" he asked.

"It's all about priorities. You needed to get well," she said.

He shot her a disapproving look. "I'm well. Look at me."

"Bet you'll need a nap by late afternoon," she said.

"You're a pain in the butt," he said. "What can I do for you? Looks like you've got an assignment to complete."

"I do," she said. "You've already done enough. I love the smell of this cappuccino, and I'm really going to love the taste of it. So go home and rest."

"I'm too bored for that," he said.

She raised her eyebrows. "Well, now we're too bored," she said with a smile.

He smothered a grin. "I am."

"I'll bore you even more if you stay. Plus I won't be able to concentrate with Mr. Hot G.I. Joe sitting next to me."

He gave a slow grin. "You're good for my ego."

"You're bad for my concentration," she said. "Shoo."

"Shoo?" he echoed as if the word didn't compute.

"Shoo," she said. "As in fly. As in I'll never get my work done if you stay. But come back in three hours if you're not busy."

"We'll see," he said and left the library, feeling her staring at his back.

Three hours later, Angie greeted him by clapping her hands together. "I. Am. Done." She turned to beam at him. "I can't believe I did it." She stood up. "Yay. Yay. Yay. Now, tell me. Did you stay awake that entire time or did you take a nap?"

"Awake the whole time," he said, scowling.

"Hey, I would have taken a nap if I could have. How did you stay awake?"

"Top secret military methods," he said.

She leaned toward him. "Spill."

"Stuck my head out the car window. Rubbed snow on my face," he said.

She laughed. "Oh, there's nothing secret about that. Let's celebrate."

"How?" he asked.

She lowered her voice. "Vegas, baby," she said with an outrageous gleam in her eyes.

He felt his gut clench. She was getting to him. He'd tried to keep himself distant from her, but after she'd come to the rooming house when he'd felt like crap, he couldn't stay away from her.

"You've never been to Vegas," he guessed.

"All the more reason that I should go," she said with a smile. "But my second choice is ice cream."

He shot her a sideways glance. "It's freezing," he said.

"I want a hot fudge sundae."

He nodded. "Game on. Nuts or not?"

"I want it loaded," she said in a sexy voice.

Forrest wanted to give it to her loaded, but at the moment she was talking about ice cream. He would pull back after today, he promised. Tomorrow. Definitely tomorrow.

Moments later, they entered the doughnut/ice cream parlor and Angie placed her order. "Two scoops, one vanilla, one chocolate, hot fudge sauce, nuts, whipped cream and two cherries."

The server smiled. "And you, sir?"

"Vanilla soft serve in a sugar cone," he said.

Angie stared at him in disapproval. "Vanilla?"

"Simple pleasures are the best," he said.

"But *vanilla?*"

"It's always been my favorite. It's come in handy when only one flavor is available."

"But the sugar cone is a major treat," she said.

"Yeah. The sugar cone is rare. And I'll be drinking coffee in a couple hours to recover from the sugar dump."

"Well, don't choke down that sugar cone just for me," she said with a laugh.

He lifted his eyebrow. "You're tough."

"I make it hard to be righteous, Major, don't I?" she said when the server handed her the loaded sundae. She stuck her spoon in it and then put it in her mouth. "Mmm."

He felt a rush of heat spread through his body. Her mouth was damn tempting and he shouldn't be tempted. More importantly, he shouldn't act on his temptation. Angie just reminded him that he was a man. With needs. But she was the wrong kind of woman. He shouldn't and wouldn't take advantage of her.

"Yes, you do make it hard to be righteous," he said when the server handed him his ice cream cone. He hoped the frozen ice cream would cool him off in every way, but he was pretty sure it wouldn't. He led her to a table by the window. "Some people would think it was crazy for us to be eating ice cream when there's snow on the ground."

"Some people wouldn't be from Montana," she said. "You gotta make the happy happen when you can."

He met her gaze and bit into his sugar cone. "I haven't heard it put quite that way before."

She shrugged and took another bite of her sundae. "It's just another way of grabbing the gusto," she said and took yet another bite.

"What made you have that kind of attitude? Not everyone does," he said and took two more large chomps of his cone and finished the treat.

"My sister and brother didn't really have the opportunity to go for the gusto once my mom died. Not until I grew up. Then they found their perfect someones and married them," she said.

"Perfect someone?"

"Your perfect someone is that person who makes you feel loved and inspired. Your perfect someone is that person you can't turn away from, no matter how much you might try."

As she looked into his eyes, she was so passionate she left him speechless. This was the girl who joked and made him laugh, but she meant business about the perfect someone. He could tell she wouldn't back down from her opinion.

He cleared his throat, "I think I'll grab some water," he said and went to the counter for a cup. He gulped down the first cup, got a refill and returned to the table.

Angie had made headway on her sundae.

"You're doing good," he said.

"Except I'm getting full," she said with a grimace.

"Take a break," he said. "The new rule is you don't have to clean your plate or bowl."

"If you say so," she said.

"I do." He glanced out the window and caught sight of his physical therapist, Kinley Smith, a petite young blonde with endless energy.

She pointed at him through the window and gave a big smile.

"Who's that?" Angie asked.

"My physical therapist," he said. "Uh-oh. Here she comes."

Kinley burst through the door and walked toward them, the hem of her coat swishing around her ankles. "There you are," she said to Forrest. "Where have you been?"

"Around. I've been busy. What about you?" he asked, fighting discomfort.

She waved her finger at him. "You were supposed to come back in for more sessions with me."

He shrugged. "I got busy with volunteer work, but I'm still working out."

"That was part of the problem," she said. "I didn't want you to damage your leg. You wanted to do too much too soon."

"I'm doing okay," he said.

"You wouldn't say anything else," she said. "You'll be seeing me again after your next surgery. You can count on it. Who's your friend?"

"Angie Anderson, this is Kinley Smith."

Angie nodded. "Nice to meet you, Kinley," she said, but her voice was reserved.

"And you, too," Kinley said. "How do you know Forrest?"

"We met when I was at ROOTS and he was walking a therapy dog. ROOTS is a local safe haven for youth," Angie said.

"I've heard about that. A great organization. Do you work there?"

"Part-time," Angie said.

"Very generous of you to work that into your schedule. It's hard adding anything to a full-time job," Kinley said.

An uncomfortable silence followed. Angie gave a shrug. "I'm finishing my degree," she said.

"Good for you," Kinley said. "Well, I should go. Enjoy your ice cream. Keep in touch, Forrest. I can help you."

"Yeah," he said. "Have a good one."

Kinley walked away and Forrest breathed a sigh of relief.

"She seemed very conscientious," Angie said.

"She is. She didn't like how much I pushed. After awhile, I decided to do my own rehab."

Angie pursed her lips. "How does your surgeon feel about that?"

"He doesn't know," Forrest said.

"That's not good," she said and took another bite of her sundae.

Forrest shrugged. "I'm doing okay. She was holding me back."

"Hmm," she said. "She sure was cute for you to bail on her."

He shook his head. "It wasn't about whether she's cute or not. It was about my progress. I just have higher goals than most people. But I respect her. She's a real professional. She has her act together."

Angie nodded. "She's educated and knows what she wants from her career." She sighed. "Must be nice."

"What do you mean?" Forrest asked, searching her face.

"I mean I'm still flailing in the wind about what I'm going to do professionally. I haven't even graduated yet. She's eons in front of me," she said glumly.

"Just because she knows what she wants to do careerwise doesn't mean she's in front of you," he said. "That's one of those things that evolves over time. Look at me," he said, pointing at his chest. "I thought I would be career army. That didn't happen."

"Hmm," she said, clearly still not convinced. "You seem to know yourself pretty well."

"I'm older than you are. I've been through more," he said, then thought about the losses she had suffered when she was young. "But you've taken some big blows."

"Still," she said. "I should be further along my career path."

He lifted his fingers to her chin. "You've got time. You're still young."

Her face fell. "Yeah, thanks," she said, but clearly didn't mean it. She dropped her spoon into the bowl of the rest of her uneaten sundae. "I think I'm done."

The mood was clearly killed. Forrest walked her to her truck, but Angie was strangely silent. "Hey, are you upset about Kinley?" he asked.

"No," she said, looking down. "She's got a lot together. It makes me think about how far I have to go."

"You don't have to go the same place she does," he said.

"I guess," she said. "I also guess I need to get moving. Thanks for the coffee and the ice cream sundae. I'll see you soon," she said and climbed into her truck.

Forrest watched her as she pulled away. He was surprised by Angie's reaction to meeting Kinley. She usually exhibited the kind of confidence that inspired others, but it seemed she felt inadequate because she hadn't fully committed to a specific career. It was totally wrong. Angie was one of the strongest women he'd ever met. She might be young. She might even be a bit naive, but she was strong.

Shoving his hands into his pockets, he walked toward the architectural office to do more work. Thanksgiving was coming and the office would be closed. He didn't want to get behind schedule. He walked cautiously, glancing around, hoping another vehicle wouldn't backfire like it had last week. When he made it to the door, he breathed a sigh of relief. Maybe he could make it through another day without a flashback.

The following Monday, Forrest met with Dr. Thomas North for a checkup. He'd been waiting for Dr. North to give the go-ahead for his next surgery. The doctor studied films and examined his lower leg. "This could require two more surgeries," the doctor said.

"Two?" Forrest echoed. He'd already been through four surgeries. He was ready to be done with this. "I was hoping I would only need one more."

"I told you it was a fluid situation and that my goal is to improve your motion and strength as much as possible." He frowned. "Are you still seeing the physical therapist?"

Forrest tensed. "I had scheduling conflicts, so I started working out on my own."

"You're right on the edge of a stress fracture," Dr. North said.

"What do you mean?" Forrest asked.

"I mean you're working that leg too hard. You need to ease off. And I'm going to warn you that you will need a brace after both of these surgeries," Dr. North said.

"Temporarily," Forrest prompted.

The doctor grudgingly nodded. "Yes, but—"

"So when can I have surgery?" Forrest asked.

The doctor shook his head. "Not quite yet. You need to back off and give your leg time to heal."

"How am I supposed to do that?" Forrest asked, completely frustrated.

"You put your leg up every time you can. You apply ice for the swelling. You walk instead of running. You baby it a little bit."

Forrest scowled. "I've been babying it."

"If you can't take the recommendations I just made, then you can use crutches or a cane," the doctor said firmly.

Forrest didn't like what he was hearing, but he knew Dr. North was his best chance at getting his leg closer to normal. "Okay, okay. But no crutch or cane."

"After your surgery, you'll need a crutch. I don't want you damaging my handiwork," Dr. North said.

"You never said when I can have the surgery," Forrest said.

"I'm gonna say after Christmas. Mid-January as

long as you don't overwork the leg. Resist the urge during the holiday season," he said.

"After Christmas," Forrest echoed, feeling discouraged.

"It's not that long. We're almost at Thanksgiving. I just want you to give your leg the absolute best chance to heal. You don't have to stop living your life. Just try not to work so hard," the doctor said.

"I've been doing that for over a year," Forrest grumbled.

The doctor nodded. "I'm going to be blunt. You almost lost your leg. You're a walking, talking miracle. I want to make you even more of a miracle. Take it easy with that leg," he said in a firm voice.

Forrest took a deep breath. "Okay. Did Annabel tell you she's loaning Smiley to a veterans support group?"

Dr. North smiled. "No, but I'm not surprised. And I gotta tell you that dog is a bed hog. If she weren't such an amazing woman," he began.

"But she is," Forrest said, seeing the love in the cranky doctor's eyes. "And you're crazy for her."

"Yeah, well," Dr. North said, clearing his throat. "I'm glad Smiley can help you out. I never thought I would say this, but I'm starting to think the dog has super powers. Don't tell Annabel I said that. She makes me eat too much crow as it is."

Forrest smiled at the brief glance into the doctor's

humanity. Dr. North was known for his tendency to distance himself from his patients. He was all about surgery, not emotion. That was why everyone had been thrilled to see him fall for sweet Annabel. She'd made him more human.

Dr. North swallowed and put on his surgeon's face. "So the rule is, if you want to have your surgery, don't strain your leg. When in doubt, rest it. I know you're a soldier, but your job right now is to protect that leg."

Forrest nodded. "I'll do my best."

"Good," Dr. North said. "We'll talk in a few weeks before Christmas. If everything goes according to plan, we can schedule your surgery."

"Okay, thanks, Doc," he said.

Forrest left the office frustrated. The doctor hadn't told him what he'd wanted to hear. He'd worked out everyday to strengthen his leg, but apparently he'd worked it too hard. Maybe Kinley had been right. But damn, she'd moved so slow. He'd been ready to scream in impatience after the fifth session. After memorizing the exercises, he figured he'd been ready to manage his recovery himself.

According to the doc, however, he needed to dial it back. Walking toward his truck, he climbed inside and stared at his leg. It was a titanium miracle encased in flesh and torn muscle.

It could have been so much worse. He could have

ended up with no leg, no life. Forrest needed to take a deep breath and work on the whole being-grateful thing. One of the guys in his support group had lost an arm. Other guys struggled with injuries. In the scheme of things, he was damn lucky.

He just knew he had to make as much progress as he could while he had the energy for it. He didn't want to be that guy who was lazy and could have gotten more use from his leg if he'd tried a little harder.

Forrest knew, however, that he had to listen to the doc. Dr. North was one of the main reasons he was staying in Thunder Canyon. He believed this doctor could reconstruct his leg to the best possible functioning level. Forrest just had to stick with him during the process. It hadn't been easy so far and it wouldn't be easy now, but he was determined.

Chapter Eight

The next day, Angie met her sister Haley for lunch. Despite the fact that Haley was the founder of ROOTS, Angie had rarely seen her sister lately. Haley was busy with fundraising, volunteer-coordination and being a wife to a millionaire. Haley's husband traveled frequently to California and Haley tried to accompany him as often as she could.

"How's it been going?" Angie asked as they sat down with their sandwiches in the coffee shop.

"Busy," Haley said. "I'd like to expand the ROOTS location, but it's in a perfect place. So that puts me in the usual quandary. Expand or find a way to meet needs within the current space. It makes me crazy, but I think we probably need to sit tight where we are and just get creative."

"The current real estate market is down. You might grab a bargain, it really depends on how many new teenagers we could be getting," Angie said. "At the same time, we could work on some other programs like sending some of the ROOTS kids to summer camp." She took a bite of her sandwich.

Haley lifted her eyebrows in surprise. "Very sensible for my little sister."

"What'd you expect? Follow Tinker Bell?" Angie asked.

Haley rolled her eyes. "Okay, okay. I underestimated you again. How's the love of your life coming along?"

Angie felt heat climb to her cheeks. Her appetite disappeared. "I'm working on it," she said. "He's a tough nut to crack. After his time in Iraq and the bad injury to his leg, he's struggling."

"That may be more than you want to take on," Haley said.

Angie bit her lip and shook her head. "No. He's worth it. It just may not be smooth sailing every minute."

Haley nodded. "If you say so. That leg injury may be the easy part," she said.

Angie frowned. "What do you mean?"

"I mean plenty of soldiers returning from Iraq also suffer from post-traumatic stress disorder."

"I've heard of that, but I don't know much about it," Angie said.

"It's rough. Flashbacks. Nightmares. It's not easy," Haley said.

Silence hung between them.

"I don't want you to get into anything you can't handle," Haley said.

Angie was immediately offended. "I hate it when you underestimate me."

"Oh," Haley said. "Sorry."

Another long silence filled the air.

"Do some research. See what you're in for," Haley said.

"Okay," Angie said while both she and her sister ate their sandwiches. Angie made it a practice to project a positive attitude and self-confidence, but lately there was one thing that had gotten under her skin. If there was anybody with whom she could trust to discuss it, that was her sister. "How bad is it that I don't totally have my career worked out?"

"Bad?" Haley echoed with a shrug. "What's bad about it? You're almost finished with your degree and you're doing awesome things for ROOTS."

"Is that what you really think?" she asked.

"I don't just think it. I know it," Haley said.

"Why are you asking that question? You've never been that concerned about having a nontraditional career path."

"I don't know. I wonder if people would take me more seriously if I had a defined career, like a nurse or librarian," she said.

"Do you think you would be happy as a nurse or librarian?" Haley asked.

"Not really," Angie said. "But—"

"But what? When you have a passion for what you're doing, you're going to be the most effective. What is this about? Do you need more money? If you do, then I can help you out," she said.

"No," Angie said, shaking her head. "I don't want you giving me money. That's part of the point. I need to be earning my own way."

Confusion furrowed Haley's brows. "But you are earning your own way. Between the admittedly small amount you earn from your work with ROOTS and your temp work, assisting the caterer, and the other stuff you do, you seem to be managing very well. Unless there's something you're not telling me. Are you sure you don't need some money?"

"No. I just started thinking about how other people often have full-time jobs when they're twenty-three," she said.

"Well, you're different," Haley said. "You always

have been. When you were young, you flitted from one activity to another like a bee going from flower to flower. I have to admit there have been times when I was worried if you were going to pass a class, but then you'd come through with flying colors. You just needed to do it your way. Right now, you're getting close to graduating, you're helping kids at ROOTS and you're spearheading several charity projects. If you want a full-time job, I'm sure you could find one. But your energy is directed in different areas, and plenty of people are benefiting from it. I don't understand why you're questioning this now."

Angie picked up a potato chip and set it down. "I don't want people to view me as less of an adult because I don't have a set job."

"What people?" Haley asked then realization crossed her face. "This is about your G.I. Joe. He's not giving you respect?"

"No," Angie said quickly at her sister's disapproving tone. "He's very respectful. He just thinks I'm very young."

"Well, you are young and you're not the most experienced woman in the world," Haley said bluntly. "But you have an incredible quality that makes people believe they can do impossible things. You've always had it. It's almost like magic, and if this guy can't see it, then he's not the right guy."

Angie bit her lip and shook her head. "He has feelings for me," she said. "It's just taking some time to come around. I'm not the most patient person, but I know he's worth it."

Haley sighed and reached out to cover Angie's hand with one of hers. "Be careful," she said. "I don't want you to get hurt."

"I'll be okay. I always am," Angie said. "On another subject, I'm bringing pumpkin pie and pumpkin chocolate chip bread to your house Thanksgiving. Is there something else I can bring?"

"I've got it all under control. Rose is bringing a relish tray and some fruit. I'll check back with you next week if I think of anything else I need." Haley glanced at her watch. "Oops, I have a meeting in ten minutes." She rose to her feet and Angie followed. "I'm glad we grabbed this time. Now don't you dare let G.I. Joe or any other man get you down," she said and gave Angie a hug.

"I won't," Angie said and couldn't help being thankful for her family. They'd allowed her to be herself and find her own way. Except for that brief period when Austin had acted out after their mother had died, Angie had always felt cared for by her sister and brother. Knowing that she was loved by Haley and Austin had made her feel strong enough to help other people. Now, though, she wanted more. She wanted a life with Forrest.

* * *

After that, everything moved into high gear. There were pies and bread to be made for the orders that had been placed. Angie held "baking parties" on Monday and Tuesday nights. Other staff and students would be on hand for the customers to pick up their ordered goodies.

Good thing because Angie would be getting ready for the holiday dinner for soldier's families. The day of the event she was so excited she got up before her alarm went off. She didn't know which she was happier about—the actual dinner or spending the whole day with Forrest. She'd been so busy she hadn't seen him in days.

After hurriedly showering and dressing, she gobbled down some leftover pumpkin chocolate chip bread and reviewed her list. Gathering a few last-minute items, she heard the doorbell ring and her heart nearly jumped out of her chest. She ran to the door and threw it open.

"Happy Thanksgiving and Merry Christmas," she said to Forrest. "Are you as excited as I am?"

Forrest grinned. "Probably not, but I'll work on it."

"This is going to be so cool," she said, gathering her bags and list. "I'm excited that Annabel is letting Smiley be there tonight."

"We just need to make sure no one feeds him. They're going to be tempted. Let me carry that," he said, taking the bags from her as they walked to his truck. "Have you spoken personally with any of the families coming tonight?"

She nodded as he drove toward the resort. "A few of them. One of the women broke down in tears. She said she'd been taking care of her sick mother and with her husband gone, she didn't know how she was going to fake being happy for the holidays for her kids. Going to the Gallatin Room made her feel as if she'd been invited to a royal ball."

His gut clenched with a strange emotion. "Like I said before, I didn't think about how hard it was for the families back in the States. If we can't bring their soldiers home for the holidays, we can at least let them know we appreciate their sacrifice."

"That's what I'm hoping," Angie said. "That, and I wish they all just have a great time tonight."

"I imagine they will," Forrest said. "It's hard to have a bad time when you're around."

Angie smiled. "Thank you very much, Major."

They pulled into the parking lot and Angie immediatcly popped out of the car. Forrest could tell she was chomping at the bit to make sure everything was in place. They entered the beautiful resort and made their way to the Gallatin Room. A Christmas tree tastefully decorated with matching ornaments sat in the corner of the room. Round tables with crisp white cloths surrounded the room in sophisticated elegance and crystal chandeliers hung from the ceiling.

"Oh, no," Angie said with a frown on her face. "This is all wrong."

Forrest looked at her in confusion. "What's wrong? It looks nice to me. It's a lot grander than a barbecue place or the mess tent where most of the soldiers will eat their meal."

"I'm not saying it's not nice," she said, walking around the room. "It just needs to be more festive. A lot more festive. We need to be cheering up these people. This is just too stuffy."

"It *is* the most exclusive place to have dinner for miles around. You're not going to find plastic blow-up Santas and snowmen."

"We don't have to go that far," she said, moving toward the tree.

"What do you mean by that?" he asked as he joined her beside the tree. The determined expression on her face made him wary.

"I mean, we can add a few decorations and it will make a big difference. But we need to go back to my house. I only brought a few things with me. We might need to pick up some lights, too." She turned to look at him expectantly. "But we need to get moving now."

And move, they did. He'd never known one person could have so much holiday paraphernalia in their attic. They quickly improvised a system of bringing down the boxes and carting them to his truck.

After the sixth trip, he lifted his hand. "You've got to be kidding," he said. "We can't need anything more."

"Just a few things," she said. "Just in case."

"In case of what?" he asked. "In case we need to decorate two more dining rooms?"

She shot a stern look at him. "That's a big restaurant. I don't want to underestimate how much I'll need to make it look festive. We don't have that much time."

"We've got more than half the day. I can come back," he said, as he watched her head for the attic again.

After loading another half-dozen boxes, Forrest was finally able to pry Angie away from the attic and usher her into his truck. He refused to ask her if she wanted to get more decorations.

"We only need to make one stop," she said, clasping her hands together and shooting him a smile.

"For what?" he asked, unable to filter his reluctance.

"Lights," she said. "It's hard not to underestimate how many lights you'll need."

"Hmm," he grunted more than said. She was going to work his butt off.

They returned to the resort and she opened the

bags from the department store where they'd stopped. "Lights first," she said.

An hour later, they'd strung all the lights from the bags and her boxes, and he was pretty sure the tree was so bright it would be picked up from satellite surveillance. They had to be done.

"Great," she said in approval. "Now the ornaments."

Forrest gaped at her. "What?"

She shook her hands in front of her expressively as if she were an artist. "We've got to make it festive."

"Okay, what do you want me to do with the ornaments? And I better warn you, if you've got tinsel, then I'm in the throw-it-on-the-tree camp," he told her.

"We'll skip the tinsel," she said. "Just put as many ornaments on the tree as possible."

"Volume," he said.

She nodded. "Exactly."

"Like the movie *Christmas Vacation* with Chevy Chase?" he said. "Loaded?"

"Yeah. Think of it as a hot fudge sundae loaded with everything," she said, and something about her expression was surprisingly sexy to him.

"Done," he said and filled the tree with ornaments while she decorated the tables.

Another hour later and Angie gave her stamp of approval. "It's perfect," she said. "It really does look like it could be in a movie."

"A scary Christmas movie," he muttered under his breath, looking at the monstrosity. "I hope all those lights won't blow the circuits."

Angie gave him a playful nudge in the ribs. "You know you love it."

"I should have brought my sunglasses in with me," he said.

"Come on, Grinch. I need to take a shower and get dressed for our event. So do you."

"What's wrong with what I'm wearing?" he asked, tugging at the button-up shirt that covered his T-shirt.

"Stop," she said, her eyes gleaming with a combination of fire and joy. "I want to double check the delivery of the gifts."

"Who is delivering?" Forrest asked. "I can do it."

She shook her head. "You need to be waiting for Smiley. One of the part-time ROOTS workers is bringing the goodies. Thanks for all your work. You put up with a lot."

He felt a rush of pleasure, but shrugged. "It was nothing."

She moved toward him as if she were going to hug him. He held his breath. Then she pulled back and clasped her hands in front of her as if to keep herself from embracing him. "It was a lot more than *nothing* for me and the people who will be coming tonight."

Silence hung between them, but it felt like a storm

cloud was coming. He could have sworn he felt a crazy electrical short zap between them. Forrest frowned at the sensation. "We should go."

Two hours and fifteen minutes later, Angie put on her mascara and lip gloss. She was wearing twice as much makeup as she ever did. It was crazy, but tonight almost felt like a date. "Crazy," she whispered to herself as she gave a second glance in the mirror and swiped her hand over her hair.

She wore her prettiest dress and hoped, for once, that Forrest would look at her as an adult. A woman he desired. It might be wishful thinking, but holidays were for making wishes come true, weren't they?

A second later, the doorbell rang and Angie's heart shot through the roof. The second time that day. She wondered if she would ever have a normal reaction when she was meeting Forrest. Angie grabbed her coat and ran to the door. Forrest, wearing his dress military uniform stared at her as she stared at him.

"You look ama—" she began.

"You look beautiful," he said at the same time.

A wave of awareness and wanting surged in the air between them. Angie could hardly breathe. Her emotions were suddenly so strong that she couldn't even speak.

Forrest cleared his throat. "We should go if we want to arrive before our guests."

Angie nodded. "Yes," she whispered, closing the door behind her and walking beside Forrest to his truck. He helped her into the passenger seat and climbed into his seat then drove to the resort.

Still stuck in that strange aura of feelings she'd experienced a moment ago, Angie struggled to think of something to say. "What are your plans for Thanksgiving?" she finally managed to say.

"Antonia and Clay have pretty much demanded that I join them for dinner tomorrow night. I've tried to give them space, but Clay says I don't need to avoid them as much as I have been."

Angie nodded. "I'm sure it's hard to strike that balance since you live so close."

"Clay and I used to eat breakfast with Antonia. I've been eating a lot of cereal to start my day lately," he said. "They're getting married on Friday."

Angie looked at him in surprise. "Really? So fast?"

He nodded. "Clay fell hard for her and he knows she's the one. With their kids being so young, they want to make it official. It won't be a big affair. A minister will do the deed in Antonia's den. They've decided to delay taking a honeymoon until her baby is a bit older. I don't mind helping with the horses, but I don't think I'm ready to take on two babies. I bet my mom is itching to get her hands on both of them, so anytime Clay and Antonia say the word, I imagine she'll be ready."

Angie couldn't help imagining how thrilled she would be to have Forrest's child. The thought conjured such strong feelings that she tried to push it away, but she wondered if their child would have his strong profile and even stronger will. One thing she knew, he would be a loving protective father. "Those kids are lucky to have Clay."

"Yeah, I wouldn't have picked Clay to jump into the fatherhood role, but he's great with kids and would do anything for them," he said.

"I didn't exactly win the lottery in the father department, so I'm always glad when I see a man step up the way he has."

"That's right. Your father left when you were pretty young," Forrest said, shooting a quick glance at her. "You don't talk about it much."

"I don't remember much about him. After he left, my mother had to work twice as hard, but she never complained, and I always felt wanted. After she died, Haley and Austin were so devoted to me. They were determined to make sure I had as normal a life as possible. For a while there, I withdrew from everyone. I was shell-shocked and I was afraid of being left behind by myself, but I came around."

"I can see why you would have been frightened.

It's a wonder you're as outgoing and trusting as you are," he said.

"I don't want to live my life being afraid," she said. "That would be a terrible way to live. There are too many happy, wonderful things just waiting to happen."

"You wake up everyday feeling like that?" Forrest asked, his voice full of doubt.

"If I don't wake up that way, then I remind myself," she said "It's not about thinking nothing bad is going to happen, because bad things do happen. I just try to fix what I can and look for the good things."

"Even when your truck breaks down in the snow and no one will pick up the phone?" he asked as he drove into the resort parking lot.

"But someone did," she said, smiling at him. "And he came and helped me."

"I can't deny that," he said as he pulled in front of the front door of the resort. "How about if I let the princess out here so you don't have to walk in the cold?"

Surprised, Angie felt a rush of pleasure. "That's nice of you, but I can walk."

"Not tonight," he said, and put the car in Park and circled to her door.

She accepted his hand as she stepped from the truck. "Well, if I'm a princess all of a sudden, then what are you?"

"The servant. The military lives to serve," he said.

With her hand in his, looking into his strong, handsome face, it was all she could do not to throw herself at him and kiss him. Angie reined in the urge. Forrest had to make the next move. She'd let him know she was interested in him since the day they'd met. It might seem like the rightest thing in the world to kiss him, but she knew she had to wait for him.

Even if it killed her.

"All right, thank you," she said and pulled away her hand. She shot him a cheeky smile. "I like a man who knows how to serve. See you inside, Major."

Angie walked into the restaurant and the sight warmed her heart. It was even more beautiful than she remembered from this afternoon. She hoped the military families would be pleased. She checked in with her contacts at the Gallatin Room. Everything was on time and under control.

Forrest followed into the Gallatin Room and nodded in approval. "You did well," he said.

"With an awful lot of help from you," she reminded him.

"I didn't do much," he said.

"Yes, you did," she said and her eyes widened as she looked at the doorway. "Oh, look, our first guests."

Angie and Forrest greeted the woman and her two young children as they walked inside the room. "Welcome to the Gallatin Room," she said and handed the woman a program. "This is Major Forrest Traub. He spent several holidays overseas before an injury brought him home for good."

The woman looked at Forrest with tears in her eyes. "Thank you for your service, Major Traub. I can't tell you what this event means to all of us."

"We're happy you could make it tonight. And thank *you* for your service," he said as he shook the woman's hand and the hands of her small children.

Angie's heart squeezed tight at his gesture. His action only reinforced what she'd known about him from the beginning, but Angie didn't have time to focus on that because the guests kept coming during the next forty-five minutes.

Finally, the families sat down to a lavish turkey dinner with all the trimmings. Everything was perfect, but Angie grew concerned about part two of this show. She glanced at her watch.

Forrest sat at the welcome table and wolfed down his plate of food while Angie didn't take a bite of hers. He looked up at her. "Why aren't you eating? This food is great."

Angie frowned. "Santa was supposed to call me when he arrived five minutes ago."

"Santa?" Forrest repeated.

"Yes. Justin from ROOTS said he would dress up as Santa and hand out the gifts to everyone along with Smiley. Speaking of which, where is Smiley?"

"He's due in six minutes. That's why I'm eating so fast. If I weren't being fed by Antonia tomorrow night, I'd ask for an extra plate."

"Yeah," she said and punched in Justin's cell number again. "No answer. This isn't good. I have the suit and gifts, but no Santa."

"Maybe he'll show up," he said and continued to eat.

Irritation nicked through her. "How can you eat when Santa may not show up?"

He gave her a blank look as he swallowed a bite. "Santa hasn't shown up for me for several years."

She scowled at him. "Then you've been hanging around the wrong people. Tonight, we have to make magic happen."

"We already have," Forrest said, rubbing his belly. "This food is pure magic."

"We need Santa."

Forrest shrugged. "Give him a little time. He is a teenager. It shouldn't be a surprise that he's late. Their concept of time can get a little shaky. Eat your dinner."

Angie dialed Justin again then one of his friends. No answer from either of them. She began to pace.

"Do you want me to tell them to wrap up this plate for you?" Forrest asked. "It would be a damn shame for you to not at least taste it."

Angie dialed Justin again and still got no answer.

Forrest glanced at his watch. "Annabel should be here with Smiley. I told her I would meet her at the front door."

At a loss, Angie followed him through the hallway. As promised, Annabel had Smiley decked out in jingle bells on his red therapy vest and felt reindeer antlers on his head.

"Oh, look at you, sweetheart," Angie said, her heart softening at the sight of the dog. She petted him on the head. "Thank you, Annabel," she said, looking at Smiley's owner.

"He's happy to serve," Annabel said. "Here are a few treats to get him through. Just try to keep people from giving him scraps. Table food is murder on his digestion."

Forrest took the leash. "Thanks. Looks like you dressed him in his holiday finest."

"He's a good guy," Annabel said and patted Smiley. "I'll pick him up in a couple hours."

Forrest walked Smiley through the hallway.

Angie couldn't hold her panic inside one moment longer. "Forrest, I need your help. I need you to be Santa."

Chapter Nine

Forrest stared at her in disbelief. "Me? Santa? Trust me, Angie, I'm no Santa."

"It's just for a little while," she pleaded.

"Two minutes is too long," he said. "You know I'm not the jolly type."

"The Santa suit will do most of the work. You can give a few ho-hos. The gifts and Smiley will distract them."

Forrest shook his head, but he felt himself weakening. Damn it.

"We can't disappoint the children," she said.

Forrest groaned. He couldn't disappoint the children. He couldn't disappoint Angie. Five minutes later, he stepped into the suit and gave himself a cursory glance in the bathroom mirror. Lord help him, he thought as he put on the hat and fake beard. He was the worst Santa he'd ever seen. He grimaced into the mirror. "Ho, ho, ho," he muttered.

He sucked as Santa, but walked out the men's room ready to rock and roll.

Standing in the hallway, Angie held Smiley's leash as the dog barked at him.

"Can't blame him," Forrest said. "I'm the biggest Santa imposter ever."

"Oh, stop it," she said. "You look great. Everyone is going to love you."

"Even Smiley's skeptical," Forrest said, lifting his hand to the dog's nose. Smiley gave it a sniff and lick of approval. The dog wagged his tail.

"He's good to go," Angie said.

"I guess I am, too," Forrest muttered and waddled down the hall.

Angie stepped in front of him and went to the front of the room to take the microphone. "Ladies and gentlemen, we are so honored by your presence tonight. We're honored by the sacrifice and service your family is making. Your contribution to our country is phenomenal and we'd like to give you a token of our gratitude. Santa and Smiley are here to help," she said and Forrest took his cue to enter the room with the therapy dog.

The crowd erupted in applause. Angie rushed to Forrest's side with one of the red bags of gifts. "Ready, Santa?" she asked.

"As ready as ever," he said. "Ho, ho, ho!"

"How are you, little girl?" he asked a girl dressed in red velvet. "That's a pretty dress you're wearing."

"Thank you, Santa," she said in a soft, sweet voice.

"Here's a little something for you," Forrest said in a gentle tone, placing a wrapped gift into her hand. The girl beamed.

He continued it over and over. Several children were brave enough to voice their Christmas wishes to him. Some whispered. The same requests were made over and over.

I wish Mommy could come home. I wish Daddy was home.

His heart broke at the words. All twenty-three times he heard them. Forrest knew plenty of kids hadn't had the nerve to ask. Instead, they'd just wished. As the realization rolled through him, he injected a little more jolly in his laughter. They needed this moment. This one evening was a holiday escape and he was damned well determined to deliver.

As they finally drew near the end of the long line of guests eager to meet Santa and Smiley, Angie noticed that Forrest had begun to limp just a little bit. She shouldn't be surprised after how hard he'd worked today. She gave another hug to another soldier's wife.

Annabel stood in the doorway ready to take Smiley away.

Forrest and Angie walked toward her with Smiley loping happily along.

"Thank you," Angie said. "He was perfect."

"Good to know," Annabel said. "We've been putting him through his paces lately and the holidays are just getting started."

"Everybody loved him," Forrest said. "You've done a good job with him."

"Smiley and I both thank you for your high praise. Now, let's see if I can keep him from being a bed hog," Annabel said with a grin and led the dog away.

The military families streamed out of the Gallatin room with smiles on their faces. As soon as the last guest was gone, Forrest went to the men's room and ditched the Santa suit. He felt a new sympathy for mall Santas. Hell, any Santas.

He stepped into the hall and walked toward Angie as she talked to a man wearing a white chef's jacket. Angie glanced at Forrest. "Forrest, this is Shane Roarke. He's responsible for the fabulous meal tonight."

"It was delicious and the families really appreciated it," Forrest said. "I thought about stealing Angie's plate, but figured she deserved a few bites after all her work. This evening meant so much to all those people who can't have their soldiers home for Thanksgiving."

Shane nodded. "You're welcome. It was my pleasure." He shrugged. "I know a thing or two about missing family," he said in a cryptic voice then extended his hand to each of them. "Good night."

Forrest stared after Shane. "There's something about that guy," he said. He couldn't quite put his finger on it.

"What?" Angie asked. "Other than the fact that he's a culinary genius and you devoured his food like you hadn't eaten in days."

He glanced at her and laughed. "Okay, okay."

They continued down the hallway and she looked up at him. "You saved the day. You were a hero again," she said with a smile that got under his skin.

He felt himself sink into her gaze. She was so beautiful inside and out.

"She's standing under mistletoe, dude," a server said as he walked passed them. "Go for it."

Angie's eyes widened and she glanced up. "I didn't—"

Forrest followed an instinct he'd been fighting for weeks. "Shh," he said and pulled her against him and pressed his mouth to hers. Her mouth was sweeter than he'd imagined; her body was softer and more sensual than he'd remembered.

He finally pulled back. "You're a very special woman," he said. "Thank you for helping me have the best day I've had since coming back to the States."

He watched her audibly swallow.

"It's not over yet," she said. "You're giving me a ride home, aren't you?"

He nodded. "Yes, I'll take you home."

Forrest drove Angie home, and it was all he could do not to grab her hand and hold it. Something in the very core of him called out to her. He wasn't totally sure how she affected him that way, but she did. He wanted to hold her tight and absorb everything that was good about her.

He arrived at her house, helped her out of the car and walked her to her front porch. Angie stood with her back to the door, looking at him expectantly. "Come inside," she invited.

"I should go," he said, but he felt no interest in leaving her.

"You should stay," she whispered.

Something powerful and inevitable kept him from turning around and getting in his truck. "Are you sure?"

She shot him the sexiest smile he'd ever seen. "I've been sure forever, Major."

His heart stopped in his chest, and he knew he couldn't turn away from her now if he'd tried. "Then let's go inside," he said.

* * *

Angie fumbled with the lock and opened the door. Forrest followed her inside. The house felt quiet except for the sounds of her breath meshing with his. He took her mouth and she felt as if he devoured her in the best possible way. Every inch of his body vibrated with honest need. Angie clung to him, reveling in the passion he was finally allowing himself to show her. Everything about him was hot, hard and muscular. Everything about him was what she'd always wanted.

She clung to his shoulders, feeling her knees turn to liquid.

He parted them slightly and she stared into his dark eyes that were full of want and need. His arms were taut around her body, although she knew he would have let her back away at any time. But that was the last thing she wanted. Angie felt as if she'd been waiting for this moment her entire life.

"Where's your bedroom?" he muttered.

Her mouth went dry. "Down the hall," she managed to utter. "In the back."

She tried to lead the way, stumbling down the hallway. They traded kisses with every step. Angie pushed off her coat and let it fall to the floor. Forrest unbuttoned his jacket. She helped loosen his shirt.

Finally they arrived in her bedroom with the queen-size bed and oak furniture. She'd never invited a man into her bedroom. She couldn't believe how right it felt to have Forrest with her tonight.

He pulled back again. This time, the space between them was a little wider. She felt a draft of cool air and uncertainty. She searched his gaze for reassurance. In that slice of a moment, she sensed that he was torn between what he wanted to do and what he felt he should do.

"What is it, Forrest? Don't you want me?"

The expression on his face looked as if he'd been pushed over the edge. "Yes, I want you," he said and guided her to the bed.

He kissed her until she was breathless with need. He stripped off her dress. Her bra and panties soon followed. She scrubbed at his chest with her fingers. She longed to feel his bare skin against hers. Pulling at his jacket, she rubbed against him.

Forrest muttered sexy sounds of frustration as he ditched his uniform and underwear. At last, he was deliciously naked with her, holding her, kissing her. Everywhere he touched her, she felt branded. He urged her down on the bed and the comforter felt cool against her back, but the rest of her was steaming. She wriggled beneath him, wanting to feel every inch of him on her, inside her.

He touched her breasts and slid his thumbs over her nipples. His caresses only served to accelerate her arousal. His hand drifted down between her legs.

"You feel so good," he said. "So good. I want you so much," he said, settling between her thighs.

He thrust inside her and she gasped at the sudden stretching sensation.

Forrest stopped short, staring at her. "You're— You haven't—"

She grasped his hips and whispered, "Don't stop. Please don't stop."

"Oh, Angie," he said and began to pump inside her. She held on as the tension tightened to the force of a tornado, her climax coming in fits and starts. He rose above her and she saw pleasure take over his face. Angie had never been so vulnerable, yet awesomely complete. She hadn't known such a feeling was possible.

Her heart hammered in her chest as she struggled for air. "Oh. Wow."

Forrest shook his head and rolled onto his side, pulling her against him. A moment of pure bliss passed. Angie was so happy she could have cried, but she didn't want to alarm Forrest, so she buried her head in his chest.

Another moment passed and she felt him take a deep breath. "Why didn't you tell me?" he asked.

"Tell what?" she returned. "That I was, uh, inexperienced?"

"Yes," he said.

She lifted her head to look at him. "Would you have gone through with it if you'd known?"

He shook his head. "Probably not."

"Exactly. That's why I didn't tell you," she said and pressed her lips against his throat. "I don't regret this. Not one bit. I'm glad you were my first."

"Oh, you're a sweetheart, but you don't know what you're doing," he said, rubbing her shoulders and holding her close to him.

"You didn't seem to mind too much," she said.

He gave a low laugh that vibrated through her. "I can't say I minded at all." He lifted her chin and gave her a long, soulful kiss that made her sink even more deeply in love with him. Angie fell asleep to the sensation of his naked body against hers, strong and loving. In her mind, their future was set.

Hours later, she awakened to the sound of Forrest screaming. Her heart leaped in a panic. He thrashed from side to side. She blinked, terrified. Was he hurt? What was happening?

As Angie became fully awake, she realized Forrest was having a nightmare. She gently tried to awaken him. "Forrest. Forrest."

Sweating and out of breath, he stared at her as if he didn't recognize her. "Where— What—" he gasped.

She took one of his hands in hers. "It's Angie," she said in a low voice as she stroked his shoulders and chest comfortingly with her other hand. "You're here with me."

A moment later, he focused on her and took a deep breath. He closed his eyes and swore.

Angie so wanted to help him. It was clear he was suffering.

"Why can't this just go away?" he muttered.

Angie's instincts went into high gear. "Iraq, right?" she asked.

He glanced at her then looked away, refusing to meet her gaze.

"Forrest," she encouraged.

But she could tell he didn't want to talk about it.

"I wish you would tell me, so I could help," she said.

"I'm okay," he said. "I'll be okay." He took another deep breath. "Just go back to sleep."

"But—"

"Not now," he said, sliding his hand behind her neck and pulling her against him. "Not now."

In the dark silence, Angie worried. Even though he was so close to her, she felt as if he had withdrawn. He had pulled into some dark place inside him. She wished he knew he didn't have to go there alone. She wished she could tell him, but he'd made it clear he didn't want her words. She was surprised he didn't abandon her in her bed. He stayed there with her and despite how upset she was, she drifted into an unsettled sleep against his chest.

Some time later, she awakened. She rolled to her side to find Forrest gone. Her stomach dipped. Sitting up, she looked around the room for him. "Forrest?" she called.

He came in from the hallway, fully dressed. "Hey," he said, leaning against the doorjamb.

She pushed her hair from her eyes. "I was afraid you'd left without telling me."

"I wouldn't do that," he said. "I'm not that bad."

"I never thought you were bad," she said and started to step out of bed when she suddenly realized she wasn't dressed. "Oops." She pulled a sheet to cover her, wishing this awkwardness between them would go away. "What time is it anyway?"

"Ten-thirty," he said.

"Oh, no," she said. "I'm supposed to be at Haley's house before noon," she said. "I would love it if you would go with me."

He immediately shook his head. "I can't make that. I really should head home."

Angie wrapped the sheet around her and rushed toward him. "What's wrong?"

"Nothing," he said. "It's just a busy day for both of us. We'll talk later," he promised and kissed her on the cheek the same way he could have kissed his sister, which was a lot different than how he'd kissed her last night.

She studied his face, but he seemed so remote. "Are you sure you're okay?"

"I'm fine." He lifted his hand to cup her chin. "Thank you for a beautiful night. Happy Thanksgiving," he said and walked outside to his truck.

Angie stared after him, hoping and praying he didn't regret their night together, but her stomach told her that he might. Biting her lip, she pushed the thought away. He'd said he was okay. She would believe him until he told her differently.

Taking a shower and packing her pumpkin pies and chocolate chip pumpkin bread, she bundled up and headed over to her sister's house. She was looking forward to the warmth she felt every time she got together with her sister and brother.

Haley's husband Marlon answered the door when she knocked and welcomed her with a bear hug. "Happy Thanksgiving, Angie. Are those pumpkin pies for me?"

Angie smiled at Marlon. He seemed like a tough guy on the outside, but he was a sweetheart to those he loved. Especially her sister. "I've brought the pies to share," she said.

He shot her a wounded look. "Well, maybe someone won't like pumpkin pie."

"Good luck," she said. "It's a great recipe. How's business?"

"Can't complain," Marlon said. "I'd like to get Haley to spend more time in L.A., but she's devoted to ROOTS. Can't fault her for that. How are you doing?"

"Good. I just finished up a charity event last night at the Gallatin Room for military families," she said.

"Impressive," Marlon said. "That's the best place to eat in Thunder Canyon."

She nodded. "It was a magical night," she said, thinking that fact was true in more ways than one. "I should help Haley in the kitchen," she said and headed for the back of the house.

Haley was stirring beans as she glanced up to see Angie. "Hey there, baby. Good to see you. Happy Thanksgiving," she said.

"Happy Thanksgiving," Angie said in return, giving her sister a big hug. "It looks like you have everything under control. No surprise there. What can I do to help?"

"You can just be your usual sweet self. Oh, I can't wait to dig into that pie," she said. "The ROOTS recipe is the best."

"That's because it's Mom's recipe," Angie said.

Haley met her gaze for a moment and Angie knew

she was feeling the same nostalgic longing. "She was a wonderful woman," Haley said.

"We were lucky," Angie agreed.

"Yes, we were," Haley said and heard the sound of the doorbell. "I believe that's our brother and his sweet bride."

"I believe you're right," Angie said.

She enjoyed the time with her family, but her mind kept wandering to thoughts of Forrest. As soon as everyone finished eating, she began to clear away the dishes from the table and started the cleanup. Haley and Rose were chatting about getting ready for the holidays when Angie started washing the pots and pans, still thinking about Forrest.

"Angie," her sister said in a loud voice.

Angie whirled around. "What?"

Haley and Rose giggled. Haley shook her head. "I've been trying to get your attention for the last three minutes. Where is your head today?"

Angie shrugged. "Sorry. I guess I'm tired from the dinner event last night."

"We should give the girl a break," Rose said. "Look at those circles under her eyes. Been burning the candle at both ends?"

Angie automatically lifted her finger to touch beneath her eyes. She rarely wore much makeup, but she realized she should have reached for the concealer this morning. "I'm sure I'll be better tomorrow."

The three women finished the cleanup in record time.

Her brother Austin appeared in the doorway. "Any chance there's more pie left?" he asked.

Rose gave her husband a hug. "You're in luck. Angie brought two."

Angie felt her heart twist at the easy affection the couple displayed. She wondered if Forrest would ever be able to express his feelings for her with such ease.

"Hey," Haley said, grabbing Angie's hand. "I wanted to ask your opinion on something for ROOTS, but I left it upstairs. Come with me. We'll be right back," she said to Rose and Austin.

"No worries," Austin said. "We have pie to keep us company."

Rose gently nudged him. "Silly."

Angie followed her sister upstairs to a small office where Haley closed the door behind them. "What's on your mind?" Angie asked.

"I'm more concerned about what's on your mind, especially after that discussion we had at lunch last week. You seem very distracted today," Haley said, and squeezed Angie's shoulder. "I'm worried about you. What's going on?"

Angie sighed and turned away. Darn Haley's intuition. Her sister had always sensed when something was wrong with Angie. "Forrest didn't just help with the dinner. He stayed overnight," Angie said and met her sister's gaze.

Haley opened her mouth then closed it. "I don't know what to say. Are you okay?"

"I'm wonderful," Angie said. "It was the most amazing night of my life, and I have no regrets. I'm just not sure Forrest feels the same way."

"Why not? From what you've said, he doesn't seem the type to conquer and disappear."

"He's not," Angie said. "I think he was upset when he first found out that I was a virgin, but we got past it. The problem was that he had a terrible nightmare. He wouldn't talk about it, but I'm sure it was about Iraq, and from the way he acted, it wasn't the first time it had happened."

"Hmm," Haley said. "I was worried about this. Post-traumatic stress disorder isn't only hard on soldiers, but also hard on everyone around them. This may be more difficult than you planned, and maybe he's not the right one for—"

Angie lifted her hand. "Don't even suggest it. Forrest is a complicated man, but he's worth everything to me. Besides, if you think about it, we're all complicated. Look at our family background. How's that for messy? How about some of the kids who come into ROOTS? How complicated are they? You haven't shied away from tough situations. Why should I?"

Haley sighed and gave a wry smile. "Because you're my little sister and I don't want you to get hurt."

"Your little sister has grown up. I'm finally in love, Haley. Don't tell me to give up on the most amazing man I've ever met."

Chapter Ten

Forrest bounced Clay's son Bennett on his knee while Antonia put the finishing touches on dinner. Antonia had timed things so that the kids would get a nap before dinner. Forrest could tell she was a natural mother and wouldn't be surprised if Clay and Antonia ended up with a whole passel of kids. If anyone could handle them, Clay and Antonia could.

At the moment, Clay was hauling the baby, Lucy, in some kind of contraption on his chest while he set the table. "Are you sure I can't help?" Forrest asked.

"You're taking care of Bennett," Antonia called. "You're helping."

A couple moments later, Antonia entered the den.

"Dinner is served." She lifted her hands to Bennett. "Let's wash our hands, big boy."

Bennett shot her a sweet smile and scrambled toward her. His nephew made some kind of unintelligible noise, but it sounded happy, so that was good enough for Forrest. He rose from the couch to go to the table and a sharp pain shot through his leg. He winced.

"Leg bothering you?" Clay asked. "You're gonna need to be careful with the holidays coming up. It will be easy for you to do too much."

Forrest knew he'd given his leg a workout yesterday for the military family dinner, but he wondered if his lovemaking with Angie added to his pain. Maybe he deserved it, he thought. What had he been thinking, getting involved with Angie? She was way too sweet and innocent for someone like him. Angie may have gone through some rough times in her life, but she didn't act like she had any baggage. Forrest had a leg that didn't work right and these damned nightmares.

He hadn't told her that the nightmare he'd had last night was hardly a one-time occurrence, but he'd been scared spitless to go back to sleep. What if he'd accidentally hurt her by thrashing around?

He'd been fooling himself if he thought something between them would work. What was worse, though, was that he'd fooled her too. She didn't deserve to have to suffer heartache because of him.

Angie kept calling him her so-called hero, but he knew the truth. There were times that he could barely hold himself together.

"Hey. Stop frowning at your plate," Clay said, drawing him out of his reverie. "You'll hurt Antonia's feelings. Act a little cheerful. At least you're getting a good meal tonight."

"Sorry," Forrest said. "My mind was on something else. The food looks great and you were nice to invite me."

Antonia entered the room with Bennett in tow. "Well, of course you're invited," she said as she helped Bennett into his high chair. "You're family. Which means you should be joining us for other meals," she said with a meaningful glance.

"I'm just trying to give the lovebirds the chance to adjust to each other. Plus, with the babies, you two need every moment you can grab together," Forrest said.

"Well, we would like some more moments with you. Stop being such a stranger," she said, putting her hand over his. "And now, let's have a blessing and eat during our babies' happy hour, which may last twenty minutes."

After dinner, Forrest returned to his suite in the boardinghouse. He wasn't tired, so he took a walk in the snow. He couldn't help remembering taking the same path with Angie when he'd been sick. Looking up at the full moon, he fought the urge to howl. He sure as hell felt like a dog. Angie deserved better, but she'd been too hard for him to resist.

He took a deep breath and remembered staring at that same moon in the Iraq desert. He shouldn't pity himself. There was someone else out there now in that desert defending our country.

Forrest sucked in another deep breath and returned home. His leg ached as he walked inside the den. A dozen football games beckoned, but his mind was too busy. His guilt was too strong. He'd taken Angie's innocence and he shouldn't have. She deserved a man who was different than he was. A man who didn't dodge bullets in his dreams. A man who didn't panic at the sound of a car backfiring.

Even after his walk, Forrest was still restless. He decided to take a hot shower and immediately turn in. Praying for sleep, he sank onto his bed and, for once, his prayers were answered.

The following morning when Forrest awakened, he knew he had to talk to Angie. He showered, fixed himself a piece of toast then called her cell.

"Hi," she said in breathy voice that grabbed at his gut. "How was your Thanksgiving?"

"Antonia fixed a great meal and the kids went to sleep early," he said.

"You lucky duck," she said with a sexy giggle.

His gut twisted again, but he knew what he had

to do. "I need to talk to you. When can we get together?"

"I'm at a retirement home right now," she said. "And I've got three more on my schedule today."

"Retirement home?" he echoed.

"Yep. I'm decorating for Christmas. Some of them are adamant that I don't put up a tree before Thanksgiving. I decorated several others a couple weeks before Thanksgiving."

Forrest looked at his den, which was completely free of Christmas decorations. "Wow. Who knew? I thought it was rushing decorations before December tenth."

"Apparently, some people agree with you. I could take a break for lunch. Would that work?" she asked.

"Yes," Forrest said. "But I have to be back for my brother's wedding."

"Oh, that's right. So exciting," she said.

"Yeah," Forrest said, but wasn't nearly as enthusiastic. "I'll meet you at noon. Where will you be?"

"Thunder Canyon Retirement Center. Please bring two sandwiches," she said.

As he drove to the retirement center, Forrest tried to put together the words he needed to say to Angie. Nothing sounded right. He picked up a couple sandwiches and walked inside, looking for her.

Forrest immediately spotted her decorating a Christmas tree in the lobby. There were enough multicolored lights on that tree to choke a reindeer. "Hi," he said.

Angie immediately turned toward him with a smile that lifted his heart and broke it at the same time. "Hi to you," she said. "And look, you brought food."

"You asked for—"

"And you delivered," she said. "Let's eat in the activity room. Despite its name, it's quieter at this time of day because everyone's getting lunch."

She led him to a room with long windows that invited the sun. Sitting at a table, she invited him to do the same. "Isn't this nice?"

"Not bad," he said and pulled out the sandwiches. "Here's yours. I took a guess and added more vegetables and less meat."

"Perfect," she said with a smile and unwrapped the sandwich. She took a bite and gave a groan. "Delicious."

"You must be starving," he said, amused despite what he needed to say to her.

"I am," she admitted and took another bite. "My sister made an amazing meal yesterday, but something strange happened and I'm hungry again today," she said, lifting her hand in consternation.

"I know what you mean," Forrest said. "Antonia prepared a great dinner last night, but now, it's like it never happened."

"What are you going to do?" she asked, lifting her fist to his for a fist-bump. Angie took several bites of her sandwich. "This is perfect."

He chuckled. "Food is always perfect when you're hungry."

She nodded and gobbled most of the rest of her sandwich. "Thank you," she said. "You saved my life."

Forrest's heart sank. She wouldn't be thinking he'd saved her life in a few moments. "We need to talk about the other night."

"You were amazing," she said. "I'll never regret that you were my first."

Forrest bit his lip. This was going to be horrible. "Angie," he said, forcing himself to do the right thing. "What we did that night—"

His cell phone rang. Forrest glanced at it and saw his brother's number in the caller ID. He swore under his breath. "Sorry, just a minute," he said and answered the phone.

"Forrest, I need your help," Clay said. "We just heard from the minister who agreed to marry Antonia and me. He's stuck in Kansas. Antonia is freakin' out. I've never seen her this way," he said in a low voice. "We need to find another minister or go to the justice of the peace."

"Give me a couple minutes and I'll call you back. Let me see what I can do," Forrest said.

"Don't take too long," Clay said.

"I won't," Forrest said and hung up. "Do you know anyone who could conduct a marriage ceremony for my brother and Antonia?"

Angie blinked. "What happened?"

"The minister is stuck in Kansas. We need someone else. Today."

"Give me a minute," she said, putting her finger to her mouth as she searched her mind for a long moment. "I have an idea," she said. "Let me make a call." He watched her punch in a few numbers. "Mary, how are you?" Silence followed. "Just curious. Do you still have your license to marry people?"

Silence followed again. "Great," she said, glancing at Forrest and nodded.

"Can you do a marriage ceremony this afternoon?"

Angie ended the call and turned to Forrest. "Mary Hillbocken will conduct the ceremony in an hour, but you have to go to her house."

"Hillbocken?" Forrest echoed. "Where does she live?"

"About an hour outside of town," Angie said. "She's a little kooky, but she can get the job done as long as you have the license taken care of."

"That's all good," Forrest said. "I'll call Clay."

"And remember, you'll need two witnesses. Mary only has cats and sheep. Lots of cats and sheep."

Forrest nodded. "Then plan on being a witness," he said. "I don't think a sheep or cat can sign."

Two hours later, Clay, Antonia, the two babies, Forrest and Angie stood in the living room of Mary Hillbocken's house. Mary owned ten cats and thirteen sheep. She was a sweet eighty-six-year-old lady with the legal ability to marry people. Dressed in fatigues and lace, she was ready to do her job today.

She cackled as she saw Angie. "Good to see you, girl," she said. "It's a good day for a wedding today, isn't it? Thanksgiving day," Mary said.

Angie hugged the woman. "Day after Thanksgiving, Mary. You should be shopping today."

Mary shook her head. "I only shop online these days. Now, are you getting married?"

Forrest gulped. "My brother and his fiancée," he quickly corrected.

"And look at those little babies. What a fine life you'll have," Mary said.

"Thank you, ma'am," Clay said. "We appreciate you coming through at the last minute."

"My pleasure," she said. "You're a lovely couple. Let me get my robe for the occasion."

She left the room and returned a few moments later wearing a black robe and carrying a book. She brought a sheet of paper inscribed with calligraphy. "I can fill in your names after the ceremony. Do you have a preference for your vows?"

"We're happy with traditional vows," Antonia said as she jiggled her baby, Lucy. "Without the obey clause, of course."

Mary cackled again. "I never include that one," she said. "Unless the husband wants to make the promise."

Clay nodded as he held Bennett. "Tradition works for me."

"Okay, then, have your witnesses hold your babies during the ceremony. I want your full attention on your oaths," Mary said.

"Yes, ma'am," Clay said and handed Bennett to Forrest. Antonia handed off Lucy to Angie.

"We are gathered here together to join a man and woman in holy matrimony. It is one of the most holy, amazing events that can occur in our world, past and modern…"

Forrest held his nephew as Mary continued the makeshift ceremony. Despite the sudden nature of the event, the woman made it feel special and intimate. She mentioned the children and their future.

"And our beloved witnesses, Forrest and Angie, I charge you with supporting this loving couple and their family as they face their challenges and joys."

Mary then continued to lead Clay and Antonia in their vows.

"I love you," Antonia said impulsively.

"I love you," Clay responded.

Forrest felt his chest grow tight at the emotion that flowed between his brother and Antonia. Bennett began to squirm.

Mary smiled. "I now pronounce you husband and wife," she said. "You may kiss your bride."

Clay pulled Antonia into his arms and kissed her passionately. She returned the kiss. Bennett babbled in happy delight while baby Lucy snored. Forrest couldn't help glancing at Angie. She was swiping tears from her eyes as she swayed from side to side with the baby.

Her response grabbed at something deep inside him. He wondered how he could possibly tell her what he needed to say.

Clay turned around with a huge smile on his face. "We're married!"

Mary apparently kept champagne around for the purpose of celebrating weddings. The eighty-six-year old woman popped the cork on a bottle of Dom Pérignon. "I'm not sure we can afford this," Forrest said to Angie.

Continuing to sway, Angie moved toward Mary and took the woman aside. After a moment, Angie waved her hand toward Forrest in an all-clear sign. Angie moved to Forrest's side. "She says it's on the house. Mary says she doesn't usually get two babies. Can't beat two babies."

Bennett complained to be released and Forrest

held his nephew's hands and walked him around the room. Everyone except Forrest and the babies drank champagne and that was okay with him. The joy of the occasion permeated the air that he breathed, and he couldn't have been happier for his brother.

Forrest just wished he could be more normal. Less messed up. Then maybe he could have the same experience with Angie. Well, minus the babies. But maybe later, he fantasized.

Forrest shut down his thoughts and focused on taking care of Bennett. Finally, Clay decided it was time to go. Mary enscribed Clay's and Antonia's names on the marriage certificate.

Moments later, Forrest and Angie helped tuck the babies into their safety seats in Clay's truck. Forrest stood with Angie and watched as the newly married couple drove away.

"That was so sweet," Angie said, swiping at her wet cheeks. "It was the sweetest wedding I've ever witnessed. It was the anti-show of what everyone else makes a show."

Forrest nodded. He needed to talk to her. But it couldn't be now. "Thank you for coming through with someone to marry Clay and Antonia."

Angie nodded. "Mary's the best."

"How do you know her?" he asked.

"I met her through a charity group I was working for in high school. We visited elderly people in the hospital. We thought we were going to lose her, but she came through. She never forgot me," Angie said.

"I understand that," he said, looking at her. "I can't imagine anyone ever forgetting you."

Angie met his gaze and smiled. "Thanks. Do you want to grab some hot chocolate or a snack?"

Forrest shook his head. "I need to get back to the ranch. Clay and Antonia will be busy if they can get those babies to sleep. I'll take care of the horses."

Angie nodded and squeezed his arm. His heart leaped at the touch. He wondered if she had a clue what kind of effect she had on him.

"You're a great brother," she said. "There you go being a hero again."

Forrest frowned. "I'm not all hero, Angie. I'm just a regular guy."

Angie shook her head. "You may deny it, Forrest, but you're a hero in a million different ways and I've got witnesses."

Forrest had his own internal witness that told him he was just a man, but he couldn't argue with her. But soon, he would have to tell her.

Angie tugged him toward her and kissed him. The caress rocked him all the way down to his toes. "Call me," she said.

Angie drove back to town after the wedding. Nothing could have topped her day, her year, like being a part of Clay and Antonia's wedding. With the babies squirming and the way Mary had proclaimed the two husband and wife, Angie couldn't recall feeling better about a couple's future. And maybe after Forrest absorbed it all, he would think about spending his life with her. She hoped he would. She hoped he would see the love they could share and the possibilities of their future.

She couldn't help thinking about their wedding. She didn't care if it was grand or small. She only knew she wanted to belong to him. Forever. She wondered if her children would look like him. She wondered if they would carry his determination. Angie knew she would love to give him children. He would be the best father ever. The father she'd never had. The father every child deserved.

Angie finished decorating the tree for the senior center, then went to the mental health facility she'd scheduled for the same day and decorated a tree for them, too. Afterward, she grabbed a take-out meal and headed home. Her meals during the two previous nights had been far different than the burger and fries she grabbed tonight.

Walking into her house, Angie was acutely aware of Forrest's absence. He had made her house feel like a home again. He'd held her and made love to her. Forrest had no idea what kind of magic he created just by his presence. His strength inspired strength in others. He was one of those rare people who gave other people power just by his presence.

Angie knew she was the woman for Forrest. She pictured their future full of happiness and children. If they had a boy, she would want to name him after Forrest. If they had a girl, she would want to name her after her mother. Their life would be wonderful. She didn't need perfect. She just needed Forrest and the love they shared. After the night they'd shared and Clay and Antonia's wedding today, she hoped Forrest knew that what they had together was most precious.

That night, Forrest didn't sleep well even though he was exhausted. He tossed and turned, wondering what to say to Angie. He felt as if he'd betrayed her by taking her to bed and not telling her about his secret disability. His limp revealed the problem with his leg, but he did his best to keep his other problem secret. How could he possibly explain it to a sweet woman who'd never been in a war zone?

He drifted into a restless sleep for a couple hours, but awakened before dawn. Forrest couldn't tolerate his thoughts, so he rose from his bed and took a shower to clear his head. He had to talk to Angie and he had to do it today.

Forrest ate toast for breakfast again, and tried to fill the time. He turned on the television, but there were no football games yet. Using the remote to flick through several stations, he finally landed on the history channel. It offended him the least. He waited until nine o'clock to call Angie.

She didn't answer, but called him back an hour later. "Crazy morning. I've been at ROOTS and they're working on their correspondence with the soldiers. We're sending out cookies."

"Good for you," he said. "You want to meet for lunch?"

"That sounds good. Anywhere special?"

"I think the diner will work," he said.

"Okay," Angie said. "Twelve o'clock?"

"Yes. I'll meet you there."

Hours later, he met her at the diner where they'd shared hot chocolate so many times before. The sweet nostalgia bit at him. Soon, there would be no more nighttime meetings. As Forrest and Angie sat down for lunch, he realized he needed to wait to *really* talk to her, so their meal was filled with mindless conversation. The whole time, however, he knew what was coming.

"This week has been crazy," she said as their order arrived. "Pies and pies and pies and the dinner at the Gallatin Room, then our night together," she said, her cheeks blooming with color. "Then your brother's wedding and, whew, nonstop decorating for me. How are you?"

"I'm okay," he said. "I'm great. How's that grilled cheese sandwich?" he asked, diverting the attention away from himself.

She smiled. "Perfect. It's a perfect grilled cheese sandwich."

Forrest tried to focus on his time with Angie because he knew everything would change after today. He had no appetite for his club sandwich and asked the server to pack his lunch in a to-go box.

"You didn't eat much," Angie said. "Is something wrong?"

Forrest shrugged. "I have a lot on my mind. Let's go out to my truck."

Angie studied him and her brown eyes turned wary. "Okay."

A few moments later, Forrest paid the bill, then led Angie to his truck.

"It's a little chilly in here," she said, bundling her coat around her.

Forrest turned on the engine. "Maybe this will help."

"What's on your mind?" she asked.

"A lot," he said and took a deep breath. "We can't see each other anymore."

"What?" she asked, her expression incredulous. "What are you talking about? Was I that bad at making love?"

Forrest swore under his breath. "Hell, no. You

were the best. You were incredible. You made me feel things I hadn't felt before."

"Then why? I don't understand."

"You're a beautiful girl, and you deserve more than I can give you," he said.

She frowned at him. "What are you saying?"

"I can't do this anymore," he said. "It's not about you. It's me."

Hurt and disgusted, Angie stared at him. *"It's me, not you,"* she repeated. "Surely you can come up with something better than that."

She could hardly believe him. How could everything go from blissfully perfect to *over* in sixty hours? She quickly moved from hurt to furious. "When did this suddenly come to you? After you'd slept with me?"

"I'm doing you a favor," he said. "We may be having fun right now, but in the long-term, getting involved with me would not be anything like the fairy tale you imagine."

Angie frowned at him. "I'm not that naive. I don't expect a fairy-tale life. If you think about my history, then you'll realize that I haven't lived one."

"Tell me you've never envisioned the wedding gown you would wear at our wedding," he said.

"No, I haven't," she told him. "I've been too busy falling in love with you."

He looked as if she'd punched him, and Angie was

glad, because he seemed to have no idea how much he had injured her.

"Just tell me, have you named the children we would have?" he asked.

Angie closed her eyes. "You bastard," she whispered.

"I'm only telling the truth," he said. "Angie, I'm telling you the truth. You're perfect the way you are. I wouldn't ever want to change you. Believe me when I tell you, this is for the best."

Chapter Eleven

The next day, Forrest's words echoed inside Angie's head and heart. He was ending their relationship before it really got started. The reality hurt so much she almost couldn't bear it. It was all she could do to get out of bed, but she had no choice. Today she had to help the ROOTS kids put together the rest of their packages for the G.I.s overseas. This particular task was especially bittersweet since she'd consulted with Forrest on the program.

Angie forced herself to present a cheerful front for the kids, but it was hard. She knew he was *the one*. But now that he'd flat-out rejected her, she was at a loss. She didn't know what to do.

If that weren't bad enough, now that Thanksgiving was over, the whole town was getting in gear for Christmas. The streets of the town were draped in holiday lights and carols were wafting from storefronts.

Angie was usually the first person to want to celebrate Christmas, but she was finding it difficult to get in the spirit now that Forrest had turned away from her. The last time she'd felt this low during the holidays had been ages ago. The first year after her mother had passed away.

She couldn't go back to being that sad little girl. Celebrating Christmas and being happy was one of the best ways she had to honor her mother, and she couldn't allow her misery over her breakup with Forrest to keep her from the joy of the season, even though she felt anything but joyful.

Angie put up her tree and decorated her house. Although the sight of her decorations did nothing to lift her spirits, she told herself that one of these nights when she turned on the lights, she would feel a little more merry. In the meantime, she needed to get ready for exams.

Forrest was miserable, but he knew he'd done the right thing. He couldn't put Angie through his turmoil. It would tear him up to see her belief in him crumble before his eyes. She had no idea how much he struggled with his memories from Iraq.

When Forrest refused to join Clay and Antonia for a meal, his brother surprised him in his den. "Since Mohammad won't come to the mountain, I thought I'd better come to you," Clay said. "I brought a casserole that Antonia baked for you. It's in the fridge."

"Thanks," Forrest said. "But she didn't have to do it."

"She wouldn't have to if you'd join us for dinner once in awhile. What's up with you?" Clay asked. "You've been acting even more standoffish than usual lately. Did you get some bad news from the doctor?"

"Nothing that bad. I'm probably going to have to have more than one more surgery and he told me to rest it more, but it could be worse," Forrest said, heading to the kitchen to grab a glass of water.

Clay followed him. "Does this have anything to do with Angie? She seemed pretty attached to you during my and Antonia's wedding. Even Antonia said the two of you would make a great couple."

Forrest felt his gut clench, but he just waved his hand. "There's nothing there. She's just a kid."

"She didn't seem like a kid to me," Clay said. "Seemed nice and pretty to me. But maybe you're too cranky to notice stuff like that lately."

Forrest scrubbed his jaw. "Give it a break, Clay. I'm not in the mood for this."

"Hey, we're just shooting the breeze. We can talk football if you like," Clay said.

"This isn't a good time," Forrest said. "I have some work to do."

Clay sighed and hooked his fingers in his pockets. "Okay. Let me know when you're feeling more sociable. And if I don't hear from you in a couple days, I'll be back."

Forrest watched his brother leave then growled at himself. He had to get out of this funk. He had to stop thinking about Angie. He'd done the right thing. He had to keep reminding himself of that fact even though he couldn't remember being this miserable. Not even after he'd first been injured. At that point, the doctors had kept him medicated so he wouldn't feel any pain. When he'd begun his recovery, he'd been grateful to have a goal.

Now, he had a goal, too. To rest. Resting was the last thing he wanted to do. He didn't need any extra time to think. Thinking just reminded him of his comrades who hadn't made it out alive. It made him wonder why he had lived and they hadn't. Lord, he was morose, he thought. The inactivity was driving him crazy. That and feeling like he needed to stay away from ROOTS. Somehow he'd grown attached to those kids.

He supposed he could go back into town and do some work at the office. Maybe it would take his mind off himself. He could only hope. On his way there, he stopped by the library to remind Annabel to bring Smiley to the next veterans support group meeting.

Smiley rose from the floor to greet him. Forrest petted the dog and waved at Annabel as she walked toward him. "Hi there," she said. "How are you doing?"

"I'm fine," he said. "I just wanted to remind you about the veterans support group meeting."

"I wouldn't forget," she said. "Smiley wouldn't let me."

The dog brushed up against Forrest as if he sensed something was wrong.

"He's giving you some doggy loving today," Annabel said. "He usually only does that for people who are sick. You don't have a cold or anything, do you?"

"No. I had a virus a couple weeks ago, but I'm healthy as a horse now," Forrest said and petted Smiley again. "I'll see you and Smiley on Thursday. The vets really like him."

"See you Thursday," she said and watched Smiley rub against Forrest again. "Are you sure everything's okay? Smiley has great instincts about these things."

"I'm okay. Really," Forrest said and walked out of the library. Even the dog could tell he was down, he thought. The downtown parking was crazy with everyone in their pre-Christmas rush, so he wouldn't be able to get close to the office. He heard the sound of Christmas carols as he walked along the sidewalk and thought of Angie. She would love this. Love the gaudy decorations. Knowing Angie, she would try to add more.

Forrest stopped short. He had to quit thinking about her.

Thursday arrived and it was time for the veterans support group. He wasn't in the mood to do as much talking today. He hoped the other guys would lead off this time.

One young man named Ben who petted Smiley spoke up. "Does anyone else have trouble with holidays? I know I should be glad I'm home, but I can't help feeling guilty. I get to be with my family when other guys are still stuck overseas."

"I know what you mean. I helped out with a special dinner for military families whose soldiers will be away for the holidays. It reminded me that it was hard for the folks at home, too," Forrest said.

"Yeah," Ben said. "My wife keeps telling me that, but she can't understand why I get down sometimes," he said.

Another man, David, nodded. "It's hard because I'm different than I used to be. I hear loud noises and sometimes I break into a sweat. Other days are so bad I have a hard time leaving the house. My wife tries to understand, but I know it's hard on her."

An older man chimed in. "I remember being shipped out, not knowing if I'd ever see my wife and kids again."

"Well, if we're gonna talk about women, I remember putting off marrying my girlfriend because I didn't think it would be fair to her if I died over there," another man named Roger said.

Forrest was moved by the men's openness. "Have the women in your lives been able to accept you now that you've come back and you're a different man?"

"My wife has. Even though I freak out over things that seem weird to her now and then, she says she's glad I'm home with her," David said.

"Coming back, I realize more than ever what a harsh world it can be," Ben said. "It makes me appreciate my wife that much more."

"My situation is different," Forrest said. "I wasn't married or involved when I was overseas, so the woman I know now didn't know me before. She hasn't experienced *normal* with me. I just don't see how it can work out."

"Depends on the woman," the older man said. "Some are stronger than others. What's yours like?"

"She's not mine," Forrest corrected.

"Well, it sounds like she's got your attention," David said.

"She does. She has." Forrest gave a dry laugh. "I'd have a hard time ignoring her. She blew into my life like a tornado."

"Troublemaker?" one of the men asked.

Forrest shook his head. "No. She hasn't had the easiest life, but she's the happiest person I've ever met. She works with teenagers and isn't afraid to step up and protect them. I don't see how she does everything. I swear that woman seems like she can be in three places at once."

"How does she act toward you?" Ben asked.

Forrest's chest went tight. "She calls me a hero, but she's the one who makes things better for a lot of people."

"Sounds like a keeper to me," the older man said. "You shouldn't let that one get away."

"Yeah, and it sounds like you're the one who has a hard case of hero-worship for her," David said.

"I don't want to put her through my mess," Forrest said. "I broke it off last week."

"Or were you afraid she would break it off with you down the line and didn't want to risk it?" David asked. "That's what I did. Luckily, mine took me back."

"For a long time, I felt guilty about being happy when so many of my buddies didn't come back. They didn't have a chance to be happy. Why should I?" the older guy said. "My wife sat me down and told me that I owed it to my buddies who didn't make it to live my life to the fullest. She's a damn smart woman. It's a wonder she married me."

Forrest felt as if he'd been hit with a two-by-four. He realized that he had in fact felt guilty about the prospect of being happy. "I hadn't thought of it that way. I've been making anyone who gets too close to me pretty miserable."

"Yeah, my wife says I'm a pain in the butt sometimes, too," Ben said. "But she wants to work it out with me. It sounds like you've found someone who wants to work it out with you. You might not want to let her get away."

After the meeting ended, Forrest mulled over the possibility. Was it crazy for him to believe he could build a life with Angie? His heart began to pound in his chest. Would she be able to handle his PTSD? He remembered the night they'd shared. She hadn't seemed terrified. She'd been concerned, but she hadn't wanted him to leave. She'd wanted him to stay.

Walking to his truck, he sat down and tried to figure what to do. He had to see Angie and try to explain. He had to see her so he could tell her that he loved her.

Angie put on Christmas music after she arrived home. She also heated the spiced apple cider she'd picked up at the grocery store. If she surrounded herself with the sights, sounds and scents of the season, she hoped she would feel a lot more jolly. She'd been hoping and wishing that Forrest would reconsider and come back to her, but with each passing day, her hope dimmed a little more.

Deliberately pushing the thought from her mind, she decided to put out a few more Christmas decorations. She pulled out a ceramic Santa candy holder and rummaged in her cabinet to put some treats into Santa's bag. "Ho, ho, ho," she said and smiled as she remembered how much she'd enjoyed stealing a few pieces of candy from this same Santa when she was much younger.

The doorbell rang and she lowered the volume of the Christmas music. Wondering who it was, she walked to the door and was shocked to find Forrest standing on her front porch. She threw opened the door and stared at him. "Hi," she managed to say through the suddenly tight feeling in her throat.

"Hi, Angie," he said, and she noticed he carried a small colorful gift bag. "I hope it's okay that I didn't call first. I wanted to bring you an early Christmas gift."

"You didn't have to bring me a gift," she said.

"Yes, I did," Forrest said. "Can I come in?"

Confused, but thrilled to see him, she stepped

aside for him to enter. "Sure. Would you like some spiced cider?"

"Not really," he said. "I want to talk to you."

Her stomach jumped with nerves. He seemed so intent and focused. She was afraid of being hurt again. He'd already broken up with her. What else could he do? she reminded herself. "Okay," she said and led the way to the sofa.

He sat next to her and gave her the gift bag. "I'd like you to open this."

Still confused, but curious, she opened the bag and pulled out a beautiful ceramic ornament of a prince and princess. "It's lovely. What made you choose this for me?" she asked, even more curious now that she'd seen the gift.

"There's a story that goes with this ornament. There was once a beautiful princess and a man who wanted to be her prince. The man looked like a prince on the outside, but on the inside he felt like a frog, or worse, a beast. He was sure that he wasn't worthy of her and he was afraid that, once the princess saw his true form, her love would tarnish."

Angie knew that Forrest was talking about himself and her as his princess. She put her hand on his. "I see you for who you really are, Forrest."

He took a deep breath. "Let me finish. The princess told the prince that her love was everlasting, regardless of the prince's ultimate form. And the prince believed her. And she made him want to believe in fairy tales and happy endings."

"And how does the story end?" she asked.

"The story isn't over yet," Forrest said, taking her hands in his. "You and I get to write this ending. But I'll tell you what I do know. I'm sorry for hurting you. I love you and I never want you to doubt how I feel about you. I have more surgeries to face and I jump at loud sounds sometimes. I don't have nightmares every night, but I have them every now and then. I'm no bargain right now," he said. "But I can't turn away from the best thing that's ever happened to me."

Angie's eyes welled with tears. She had only dreamed of Forrest confessing his love to her. She almost couldn't believe her ears. "Forrest, I love you too and I don't ever want you to doubt that."

"It won't always be easy," he said.

"I know that," she said and lifted her hand to his strong jaw. "But we are so much better together than we are apart. You are my special someone."

"For a while, I didn't believe there was a special someone for me. You've changed my mind."

"Oh, Forrest," she said and put her arms around his neck. He pulled her against him in the most wonderful embrace she'd ever experienced. Then he lowered his head and kissed her. The raw emotion in his caress made her cry.

He pulled back and touched her wet cheek. "Why are you crying?"

"I'm so happy," she said. "You've made me so happy."

"I'm just getting started," Forrest said.

She looked down at the ornament. "Let's hang it on the tree," she said. "It will be my most precious ornament because it will remind me of your love for me."

They both rose and hung the ornament on the front of the tree.

"Can you stay awhile?" she asked.

He nodded. "You might have a hard time kicking me out."

"There's no danger of that," she said.

"I'll build a fire," he said.

"I'll get the cider and some cookies," she said.

Moments later, they settled in front of the fire and Angie leaned her back against Forrest's chest. She felt him sigh in contentment and the sound rippled through her. He was such an incredible man. She wanted him to never forget it. She wanted him to know that he could count on her.

He nuzzled her neck and she felt a rush of sensual awareness. Turning to face him, she met his gaze. "Do you know what I've never done?" she asked with a smile.

"What?" he asked, pushing a strand of hair from her face.

"I've never made love in front of a fire," she said.

His dark eyes lit with twin flames. "Is that so?"

She nodded.

"I can help you take care of that," he said and pulled her on top of him. He took her mouth in a deep kiss that seemed to go on forever. She just knew she didn't want him to stop. "You feel so good," she whispered when he pulled back for air. "Your mouth, your chest, your—" She paused. "Your everything."

He smiled at her words. "Your everything feels good to me, too," he said and slid his hands beneath her sweater. Everywhere he touched her, her skin heated. When he removed her sweater and his shirt, she moaned at the sensation of his hard chest against her breasts. When he pushed aside the rest of their clothes, she wanted him inside her immediately.

But he seemed determined to take his time with her, teasing and taunting her in the best way possible. Finally, he positioned her on top of him and eased her down onto him. It was the most glorious sensation she'd ever had. He guided her in a rhythm that made her feel a little crazy.

It didn't take long before she felt herself going over the edge, and he followed right after. Angie sank onto his chest and struggled to catch her breath.

"Being with you was so good the first time, but it's even better knowing that we love each other."

He nodded. "You are a dream come true, Angie. My dream come true," he said.

"And you'll always be my hero," she said. "Forever."

* * * * *

Don't miss
THE MAVERICK'S CHRISTMAS HOMECOMING
by Teresa Southwick,
the next installment in
MONTANA MAVERICKS: BACK IN THE SADDLE!
On sale December 2012,
wherever Harlequin books are sold.

COMING NEXT MONTH from Harlequin
Special Edition®
AVAILABLE JUNE 19, 2012

#2197 THE LAST SINGLE MAVERICK
Montana Mavericks: Back in the Saddle
Christine Rimmer

Steadfastly single cowboy Jason Traub asks Jocelyn Bennings to accompany him to his family reunion to avoid any blind dates his family has planned for him. Little does he know that she's a runaway bride—and that he's about to lose his heart to her!

#2198 THE PRINCESS AND THE OUTLAW
Royal Babies
Leanne Banks

Princess Pippa Devereaux has never defied her family except when it comes to Nic Lafitte. But their feuding families won't be enough to keep these star-crossed lovers apart.

#2199 HIS TEXAS BABY
Men of the West
Stella Bagwell

The relationship of rival horse breeders Kitty Cartwright and Liam Donovan takes a whole new turn when an unplanned pregnancy leads to an unplanned romance.

#2200 A MARRIAGE WORTH FIGHTING FOR
McKinley Medics
Lilian Darcy

The last thing Alicia McKinley expects when she leaves her husband, MJ, is for him to put up a fight for their marriage. What surprises her even more is that she starts falling back in love with him.

#2201 THE CEO'S UNEXPECTED PROPOSAL
Reunion Brides
Karen Rose Smith

High school crushes Dawson Barrett and Mikala Conti are reunited when Dawson asks her to help his traumatized son recover from an accident. When sparks fly and a baby on the way complicates things even more, can this couple make it work?

#2202 LITTLE MATCHMAKERS
Jennifer Greene

Being a single parent is hard, but Garnet Cottrell and Tucker MacKinnon have come up with a "kid-swapping" plan to help give their boys a more well-rounded upbringing. But unbeknownst to their parents the boys have a matchmaking plan of their own.

HSECNM0612

The Bowman siblings have avoided Christmas ever since a family tragedy took the lives of their parents during the holiday years ago. But twins Trace and Taft Bowman have gotten past their grief, courtesy of the new women in their lives. Is it sister Caidy's turn to find love—perhaps with the new veterinarian in town?

Read on for an excerpt from
A COLD CREEK NOEL by USA TODAY
bestselling author RaeAnne Thayne, next in her ongoing series THE COWBOYS OF COLD CREEK

***

"For what it's worth, I think the guys around here are crazy. Even if you did grow up with them."

He might have left things at that, safe and uncomplicated, except his eyes suddenly shifted to her mouth and he didn't miss the flare of heat in her gaze. He swore under his breath, already regretting what he seemed to have no power to resist, and then he reached for her.

As his mouth settled over hers, warm and firm and tasting of cocoa, Caidy couldn't quite believe this was happening.

She was being kissed by the sexy new veterinarian, just a day after thinking him rude and abrasive. For a long moment she was shocked into immobility, then heat began to seep through her frozen stupor. Oh. Oh, yes!

How long had it been since she had enjoyed a kiss and wanted more? She was astounded to realize she couldn't really remember. As his lips played over hers, she shifted her neck slightly for a better angle. Her insides seemed to give a collective shiver. Mmm. This was exactly what two people ought to be doing at 3:00 a.m. on a cold December day.

He made a low sound in his throat that danced down her spine, and she felt the hard strength of his arms slide around her, pulling her closer. In this moment, nothing else seemed to matter but Ben Caldwell and the wondrous sensations fluttering through her.

Still, this was crazy. Some tiny voice of self-preservation seemed to whisper through her. What was she doing? She had no business kissing someone she barely knew and wasn't even sure she liked yet.

Though it took every last ounce of strength, she managed to slide away from all that delicious heat and move a few inches away from him, trying desperately to catch her breath.

The distance she created between them seemed to drag Ben back to his senses. He stared at her, his eyes looking as dazed as she felt. "That was wrong. I don't know what I was thinking. Your dog is a patient and…I shouldn't have…"

She might have been offended by the dismay in his voice if not for the arousal in his eyes. But his hair was a little rumpled and he had the evening shadow of a beard and all she could think was *yum*.

***

Can Caidy and Ben put their collective pasts behind them and find a brilliant future together?

Find out in A COLD CREEK NOEL, coming in December 2012 from Harlequin Special Edition. And coming in 2013, also from Harlequin Special Edition, look for Ridge's story….

HSEEXP1212